Ricardo's Extraordinary Journey

A Boy's Mystical Quest
for Fame, Fortune and Adventure

By Rich Bergman

D0967599

Ricardo's Extraordinary Journey

A Boy's Mystical Quest for Fame, Fortune and Adventure

Rich Bergman

AUTHORS NOTE:

This is a work of fiction. While many names, places and incidents are based in historical fact, Ricardo, his family and most of the characters in this book are products of my imagination and used fictitiously. Any resemblance to actual persons, living or dead, business establishments, events or locales is entirely coincidental. I used Wikipedia, Duckster, Encyclopedia Britannica, Quora Digest, Kiddie Encyclopedia, Booktopia, Merriam Webster Dictionary, National Geographic Kids, Ancient Origins online, Scholastic.com, and A to Z, and World History Classroom as general references for this book.

ISBN: 978-0-9903352-2-1
LCCN: 2019940522

DEDICATION

Ricardo's Extraordinary Journey is dedicated to our grand-children: Ariella, Talia, Zachary, Tamar, Hannah, Jonah, Anika and Ella. May they all experience great adventures in their lifetimes.

ABOUT THIS BOOK

The original artwork for this book was created by the following student artists at Ringling College of Art and Design, Sarasota, Florida:

Dionisius Mehaga Bangun Djayasaputra (Dion MBD)

Angie Zhaodong Rao

Alyssa Russell

Anthony Smith

Under the guidance of their professors:

Scott Gordley and Tom Casmer,

and art direction by Jennifer Bernthal

Many people helped me with editing, research and other necessary actions required to complete *Ricardo's Extraordinary Journey*. They include:

Bob Casper, Renee Crames, Brieana Duckett-Graves, Tamar Eisen, Len Glaser, Josh Gluck, Sofia Keli Lumpkin, Sunny Dali Lumpkin, Joey Mitchell, David Monforton, Zack Nusbaum, Chana Steinmetz, Rabbi Chaim Steinmetz,

Benji Wilhm, my publisher - Cindy Readnower, of Skinny Leopard Media and my patient and understanding wife, Rebecca .

Special thanks for her exceptional creativity and editing to my talented and loving daughter Julie!

Other books by Rich Bergman:

Grampa's Bicycle

Not as Much as I Love You

Rocco the Platypus Gets Bullied

Rocco the Platypus Meets Herman the Bully

Sarah Seahorse Wants a Family

Note: The letters used to start each chapter are replicas of the printmaking blocks used in the 14th century.

TABLE OF CONTENTS

THE JOURNEY HOME

HOME

PROLOGUE

"Grampa, Grampa... please tell us a story.
Tell us about Ricardo."

It was bedtime and the children had gobbled down their evening snacks, giggled through supervised tooth brushing – with Yael blowing little pink toothpaste bubbles – and now they were sitting up in his king-sized bed with its overstuffed pillows and deep blue comforter. "These are eight of the smartest and sweetest children in the world," thought their grandfather.

The children loved sleeping over at their grampa's house. There were after dinner trips to Baskin Robbins for cookie dough, butter pecan or even bubble gum ice cream. He made up all sorts of fun games – like "monster tag" – and planned elaborate scavenger hunts for their excitement. Grampa quizzed them with word games and math problems, constantly trying to encourage yet challenge them just a little.

"How much is 5+6+11-11, David?"

After some quick math, David would shout, "11!"

"How do you do that so fast?" asked Grampa, and the seven-year-old would shrug his shoulders and smile broadly, feeling very pleased with himself.

Grampa taught his grandchildren songs from the old days, like "Down by the Old Mill Stream" and the Lake View High School fight song. The children especially liked the ending, "Cha he, cha ha..." But mostly, Grampa told them stories. He spun stories of Native American spirits rising from the smoke of Wisconsin campfires, stories of meetings in Chicago with Casper and Spooky, two very friendly ghosts, and stories of the adventures of young princes and princesses from England, Spain and Russia with names like Edward, Isabella and Anastasia. The children learned about the importance of education, honor, family and love. They loved to hear his stories, but most of all, they loved the adventures of Ricardo.

"All right, Michal, settle down. Rachel, I'll tell the story if you promise to go to sleep right afterward," Grampa said softly as he gently patted the heads of his two eldest grand-daughters, while wondering who enjoyed this ritual more, the children or him.

"Grampa," asked Shira, her eyes open wide with excitement from knowing they had won ... and savvy enough to recognize now was the time to negotiate her best deal. "Can you start in the beginning, back in Spain in the 1300s?"

"Please, Gumpa," cooed Rachel using her favorite nickname for him. "We'll be here a whole week this time. If you tell us five or six chapters each night, you could finish the whole story before we have to leave. Please, Gumpa."

"What do you think, Lev?" Grampa asked. "Would you like to hear the adventures of Ricardo too?"

Lev nodded his head in agreement and his blonde hair bounced just a bit. Lev didn't like to waste words, but for a three-year-old he certainly shook his head a lot.

"Ok, here goes," Grampa began.

All eight children with Aviva and Esther, the two youngest grandchildren in the middle, laid back beneath the covers, closed their eyes and snuggled together comfortably while waiting for their grandfather's story.

"Like a beautiful painting!" Grampa thought to himself.

FAMILY

Chapter One
Alberto

he leeches attached themselves to the cuts the barber made in the pus-filled sores on Alberto's groin, chest and neck, and right before Ricardo's eyes, they grew fat with blood. This leeching process was intended to suck out *cosas malas*, or the poison, but instead it sucked the very life out of his father. Ricardo poured salt on the fattened leaches, which immediately fell away. After the treatment, it took Alberto nearly a week to regain enough strength just to wash and care for himself. Returning to work at the *farmacia* was simply out of the question.

Alberto was one of the millions of people in Europe suffering from this horrible, debilitating disease, which included sores, vomiting blood and a high fever. The doctor had informed Ricardo that this disease was called the plague, and while its cause was still unknown, there were several credible theories. He said that the plague could be attributed to "pockets of bad air; the unfavorable alignment of Saturn, Jupiter and Mars; and agents of the Devil poisoning the wells."

Ricardo later learned that the plague originated in Central Asia and was carried on merchant ships to Europe by fleas on the backs of rats and cats. The plague, also appropriately known as the *Black Death*, killed half of the people it infected, which was one-third of the total population of Europe at the time. The disease had already devastated so many families, and the Columbos were no exception.

Life had been especially hard for Ricardo Columbo's family over these past two years. Since his father became ill with the plague, things were certainly different.

Each member of the family tried to help. His mother, Marta, after a full day of teaching at the Bilbao School, began tutoring students in their homes to help make ends meet. Marta's specialty was languages, in particular French,

Hebrew and Latin, which seemed to attract the children of the wealthy families in Madrid. The extra money was not enough to make up for her husband's lost wages, so one evening she came home from tutoring with a basket of laundry on her head. She placed it on the floor, looked at her family and softly explained, "One has got to do what one has got to do." Marta proceeded to scrub each piece of clothing with determination. It was hard for Alberto to see his wife make such a sacrifice, but he was too weak to protest.

It was also hard for Ricardo. His mind switched back to a better time. He recalled the last time the family went out together for a fun evening at the theater. How he had loved that night! Alberto, Marta, Ricardo, his younger sister Anna, and his little brother Esteban were dressed in their finest clothes. Mother made a feast of baked bread, honey, spinach and even a brisket of beef. After they blew out the candles and left the house, they went to the *confiteria* sweet shop, where Ricardo, Anna and Esteban each chose a small bag of candies to munch on in the theater.

The play featured a boy who traveled the world to seek

adventure. He battled pirates, saved a town from flooding, rode elephants in India, and fell in love with a beautiful princess. The boy had kept a journal, which he read to the audience. Ricardo left the theater with an acorn of an idea that grew into a strong oak in a matter of days. He would strike out on his own great adventure. He was fourteen years old, and certain that he was ready. In a few years, he would return home with knowledge and riches that would make him famous and his family proud. This dream was shared by many young men, but experienced by few. Ricardo currently was in his third year of a pharmacy apprenticeship, and his father had a vision that one day he and Ricardo would own their own neighborhood farmacia. He even had the name picked out: Columbo Family Farmacia.

For as long as Ricardo could remember, every Sunday morning, his father would take him to the countryside to search for plants, roots, leaves, and bark with medicinal value. "These are for diarrhea, this bark will make a child vomit if they drink poison, and these leaves, when ground into a mortar with alcohol, will stop dizziness," Ricardo's father had patiently explained. Ricardo liked learning about the different plants, but most of all he enjoyed being alone with his father. It was their special time together, without brothers or sisters, adult discussions about money, or uninvited neighbors. It was just Alberto and Ricardo, the future proprietors of Columbo Family Farmacia.

But these days, the theater and the Sunday outings were distant memories. Three weeks after their theatre excursion, Ricardo's father fell ill. First there was a rash, then sores over most of Alberto's body, followed by vomiting and a high fever. Ricardo stayed home from school and from the farmacia to care for his father. He learned to soak sheets and towels in cool water, wring out the excess, and then wrap them carefully around his father's burning body. "Do this to fight the fever. If you can keep him cool, your father has a chance to live," explained the doctor wearily, as he had witnessed so many cases of the plague lately.

So, every waking hour of every day for nearly a month, Ricardo battled with the plague. It was not a glorious battle. There were no swords and shields glistening in the sunlight nor mighty steeds flying into a hoard of plundering Tartars from the North. But it was a battle just the same, and an intense and serious one at that. Ricardo's battle was fought with wet sheets, soaked towels and love. Eventually, the fever broke. His father's body was weak and ravaged by the disease, but Ricardo had won. His father would live!

To help repay the mounting family debt, Ricardo took a second job, this one in the La Latina Community Hospital. Ricardo got up every morning at four, washed, ate some bread with jam, and arrived at the hospital promptly before sunrise. When the chief nurse originally hired Ricardo, she explained that he would be a nurse's aide. The title made him feel that he would be a key member of the medical staff. His work was indeed valuable, but it was work that no one else wanted to do. Cleaning bedpans, emptying spit buckets and washing sheets covered with vomit was not exactly everyone's idea of satisfying work. Yet, somehow, Ricardo didn't mind, and within a few days he felt comfortable working in the hospital. Soon he was cleaning not only bedpans, but sores, cuts and wounds as well. The doctors and nurses liked Ricardo, and more importantly, the patients liked him. Señorita Cordoza would not let anyone else feed her, and Señor Marco waited patiently for Ricardo to give him his morning bath. "He has the touch of an angel, a gift," the Señor proclaimed one day after Ricardo massaged his sore back.

On many occasions, though he was quite tired, Ricardo would sit with a sick or dying patient and do what he did best: he would listen. Ricardo was a good listener.

Ricardo's life was very full. First, there was the hospital early each morning, followed by school, then the farmacia. The apprenticeship position had him busy until dark, as he was obligated to close up every night. Ricardo's mother kept dinner warm for him, though lately it was mostly rice and beans. He struggled to keep his eyes open for his homework, then fell exhausted into bed.

"Thank you for this, my son," Marta said as she took Ricardo's hard-earned pesos, wrapped them in her handkerchief, and carefully tied a ribbon around the bundle like a little present. Then, she placed the precious sum into her savings jar, which she hid in the pantry. Secretly, Ricardo wanted to save some of the coins for his future travels, but he saw how his mother patched Esteban and Anna's clothes and how they seemed to eat only beans and rice. Finally, when the landlord put them out of their lovely little house for being late with the rent, he simply gave every single peso to his mother.

Following their eviction, the Columbos moved to a two-room flat in a poorer section of Madrid. It was depressing at first, but when Marta took the family's bright-colored quilts and hung them on the walls, lit candles, and sang songs in her melodic voice, their rooms became a home.

Even with the sadness of the move, added responsibilities, and his father's s weakened condition, Ricardo could not stop dreaming about his great adventure. He fantasized about sailing in a huge ship to Africa, discovering diamonds, freeing the slaves in the mines, and coming back to Madrid with his pockets bulging with precious stones. He dreamed he would buy the entire run-down neighborhood, demolish it, and rebuild it with beautiful homes, schools and parks. In the middle of all of this would be the Columbo family estate. "A young boy's dream," Ricardo thought wistfully, but he was torn. "How can I leave my family when they still need me?" Yet, he rationalized that there would be one less mouth to feed. "The truth is," he reasoned, "I'll never find success here." Ricardo wondered about where he might go, when he could leave, and most of all, how he would tell his family. He finally came to this conclusion: "I will wait for a sign. Something will signal me and give me the answer."

One morning, after Ricardo had emptied his last bedpan, he walked through the ward that the nurses called "death's front porch," because it held the sickest patients, and very few ever left there alive. He stopped to sit with a young girl who had fallen into the river a week earlier and had not yet regained consciousness. She was likely an orphan, Ricardo thought, since no one ever came to visit her. Ricardo took the girl's hand and spoke softly into her ear, reassuring his silent audience that she would recover and be dancing and singing again. In fact, he felt certain that once she recovered, she would start on the path to becoming a famous actress or ballerina. The nameless girl lay with her eyes closed, never moving, barely breathing it seemed. But Ricardo felt she heard him, and once he was certain he saw a slight smile appear on her angelic face.

Chapter Two
Sénor Mateo Vasquez

icardo left the girl's side and was immediately drawn to the far corner of the ward. There, lay a wizened old man who was shivering violently. His skin was so thin that it looked like paper. Ricardo couldn't take his eyes off the man's hands – especially the backs of his hands. There, the veins were so prominent that they appeared to be raised, light-blue letters of the alphabet. The left hand looked like K I X and the right like W. Did these letter-like veins mean something? Was this the sign Ricardo was looking for?

Ricardo touched the old man's forehead; he felt like he was on fire. Ricardo ran to the water bucket, soaked a towel, and gently placed it on the old man's face. Just as he had learned to do for his father, he put a sheet in the cool water. Then he pulled back the covers, and carefully placed the wet sheet on the man's withered skin. Ricardo molded the sheet to every inch of the man's body, in between his toes and fingers, and around the back of his scrawny neck.

Ricardo even thought that he saw steam rising from the cool sheet as it hit the man's burning body. He did this again and again until finally the fever broke.

The man's shivering stopped, and he looked up at Ricardo and smiled. Ricardo felt that he had seen that smile before somewhere.

It was now late in the afternoon, and Ricardo had been at the hospital all day. He was so absorbed in his tasks that he had missed school, but still he ran to the farmacia. Once there, he told Señor Bracco, his pharmacy mentor, about the old man and asked for his help.

Señor Bracco mixed Ricardo a purple-colored concoction made especially for the plague. "Give him a spoonful every four hours, with lots of water and green tea, keep wetting him down, and make certain he keeps talking. If he falls asleep, he might never wake up. Go now, and I'll tell your parents that you returned to the hospital."

Ricardo found the old man burning hot and asleep. He shook the man to wake him, gave him a spoonful of the medicine, then a large cup of water. The old man's hands trembled as he held the cup, but he drank greedily, as if to drown the fever.

For the next three days, Ricardo stayed with him, soaking the sheets, giving him the medicine every four hours, and helping him – no, forcing him – to drink and drink some more. In those three days, the man drank forty-three cups of water.

Ricardo later wondered why, with all that water, the old man never had to relieve himself – no bedpan or sheet changes at all. "Strange, like a desert cactus," he thought to himself.

Ricardo's mother and Anna came to the hospital to deliver a little food for Ricardo, and after a few hugs, left him to his patient.

Señor Bracco arrived with more medicine, some books and a piece of candy for Ricardo. It was an orange peel covered with crystallized sugar. Ricardo savored the candy, trying to make it last by taking small bites and letting the sugar melt on his tongue and drip into the back of his mouth.

Except for the brief respites with his family and Señor Bracco, Ricardo remained by the old man's side, talking and telling stories all the while. He remembered what Señor Bracco had advised about preventing the old man falling asleep for fear he might not awaken. So Ricardo talked and talked. He recounted stories about school, his friends, his family, *futbol* and, of course, his yearning for adventure.

Finally, the old man began to speak as well, but Ricardo had a difficult time understanding what he said. "He must be delirious," Ricardo thought as he listened to the old man's tales of jungles with witch doctors, slaves in salt mines, camels, trees so large you could live inside them, and ghosts and spirits.

Eventually, the old man's eyes cleared, the fever stayed down, and his mutterings became more understandable. Ricardo and the old man's locked eyes in a quiet harmony, with the knowledge that the old man would be fine, at least for now. Both were exhausted from the days' long ordeal, and Ricardo curled up at the foot of the bed and immediately fell asleep.

When Ricardo awoke, the old man was watching him. "My name is Mateo Vasquez. I am from Sevilla," he began. And with some effort, he pulled himself up in the bed. "I am an explorer. I have discovered, mapped and claimed many islands and territories in the name of the king and queen of Spain.

"I have no friends or family left. The monarchy does not remember what I did for Spain. Thank you for helping me," said Mateo.

"I am Ricardo Columbo from Madrid," Ricardo replied. "I am a student, and a pharmacy apprentice. I work at the hospital in the mornings, which is how I found you. I also want to be an explorer. I have been waiting for a sign to begin my travels."

"You have been most kind to me. I can see in your eyes

that you are a good lad. I also sense from the way you cared for me that you are a natural healer," answered Señor Vasquez."

"I may be, but first I want to be an adventurer. I want to experience the world and its secrets. I want to earn lots of money so I can help my sick father and the rest of my family," shared Ricardo.

Ricardo took the old man's hand and continued, "Señor Vasquez, will you tell me about your adventures as a royal explorer? I will record every word, so I can remember it correctly and so that history will remember you and your accomplishments."

"How can I refuse a request from the boy who saved my life and showed me such kindness?" replied the Mateo with a warm smile.

Over the next two weeks, Señor Vasquez recounted his story in great detail – and what a story it was!

Señor Vasquez began his adventures as a ship's boy at age twelve and never stopped sailing. Much of what Ricardo had assumed were fever-fueled ramblings turned out to be true accounts of his life. The jungles, witch doctors and spirits actually happened. Ricardo wrote down each detail of Señor Vasquez' story– and more importantly, he believed every word.

Ricardo's mother invited Señor Vasquez to dinner the evening he left the hospital. The conversation was warm, and it felt like the Señor had always been part of the Columbo family. Over cake and tea, Marta invited him to live with the family for a while. After a few polite refusals, the old man gratefully agreed. "Good, then it is settled," Marta said. "You will sleep in Ricardo's bed, and Ricardo, you will sleep on the sofa." Ricardo agreed with a happy heart.

The apartment was crowded, but livable, and the children enjoyed having the Señor around. He became the grandfather they never had.

As the Señor grew stronger, so did Alberto. Was it a coincidence, the wondrous tales from Señor Vasquez, or just the tincture of time? No one knew for certain, but there was a wonderful change in Alberto and in the entire family.

ON TO AFRICA

Chapter Three
The Journey Begins

ith both his father and the Señor recovering, Ricardo felt it was now time for him to leave. He spoke to his family one Friday night after dinner. "I am fourteen and I am ready to see the world. I want to return to you educated, rich and famous."

There were tears and many hugs, but that night, as he slept, Marta filled her son's pack with bread, jelly and some dried fruit. She put in two pairs of socks, underwear, an extra shirt and his father's leather jacket. She sewed a pocket in the lining of the jacket and finished it with oilcloth to protect its contents from water. She sewed on a button for safety, and inside the pocket, she put a note wrapped around eighteen pesos.

The next morning, Ricardo's mother cooked some of their precious eggs with toast. Everyone was too sad to eat – everyone, that is, except Señor Vasquez. The Señor's body was replenishing itself, so he was always hungry. After he wiped the last crumb from the corner of his mouth, he asked for some time alone with Ricardo. They went outside to the courtyard and sat facing each other in the early morning sunlight. Señor Vasquez began to speak.

"Nearly a year ago, I was in Northern India learning about yoga and meditation. My teacher was a yoga master who could twist and bend into positions that a contortionist would envy. He was very flexible, but he was also very strong. He could do a headstand for hours on end, and with great calmness. He was able to teach me the basics of the art of yoga. I learned that yoga, like life, is a process; it takes time, energy, courage, and patience. There is never an end, but the process itself is very rewarding indeed.

"The master taught me how to clear my head of all thoughts, to cleanse my brain completely until there was nothing but space. He could fall so deeply into a meditative state that his helpers would stick long needles into his hands, feet, and even through his cheeks and he would feel no pain. I must admit I was quite impressed by this.

"One day, the master asked me to accompany him to a festival called *Kumbh Mela*. The festival is held only once every twelve years, and devotees believe that a dip in the Ganges River during the festival will wash away their sins. When we arrived at the river, we saw hundreds of thousands, maybe millions of people on the riverbanks and in the water. I watched, listened and absorbed the colorful sights, sounds and smells. I was particularly interested in the *sadhus*, Indian holy men who covered themselves in ashes, chanted and prayed in the river. Some were naked. Others wore gold, orange or red robes, and others wore only loincloths. A few had snakes wrapped menacingly around their shoulders, while others were involved in painful and risky practices. These included lying on a bed of nails, piercing themselves with blades and pins in some very strange places. One sadhu was held in the air by his beard, which was tied to a pole; still another had fingernails more than a foot long that curled like the tail of a pig. Many had bowls laid out in front of them for donations of food or coins. There were so many curious and fascinating activities that I didn't know where to look next.

"From one of the more crowded areas, I thought I heard my name being called, 'Mateo, Mateo Vasquez.' I turned and my eyes locked with those of a very small, thin sadhu, who was sitting cross-legged on a small wooden raft. Flowers were strewn around him, in the water, on the raft, in his hair and all over his body. Most of the flowers were white, but there were sprinklings of yellow, blue, red, orange and purple too. He was surrounded by a dozen or so powerfully built young men whose job seemed to be to protect him from the huge crowds. These guards allowed one person at a time to approach the holy man, whisper to him and accept his words of advice, wisdom and prayer. After each person's visit, I found the sadhu staring at me. His eyes seemed to pull me toward him. Almost in a trance, I walked into the Ganges and up to his raft. The guards opened a path for me and I was suddenly standing in front of the holy man. He looked at me in such a way that I felt he was peering into me, into my very soul. With a soft yet clear voice he said, 'Mateo Vasquez, our world needs you.'

"I was startled – no, stunned! How did this holy man, from thousands of miles from my homeland, know me? Know my name? It gave me an eerie feeling, yet somehow, I was not afraid.

"'Mateo, come sit with me. I am Asta, a sadhu, a Hindu holy man. If you listen carefully to every word I speak, you may be able to help save our sad world some day.'

"Just like you sit and listen to me, Ricardo, I did the same with Asta. For three full days, without food or water, without sleep, he talked, sang and recited ancient poetry. There was an aura of holiness about him. We discussed why some people are so angry and aggressive while others are so calm and loving. Why some are polite, yet others disrespect-ful. Why some harm our land and water, while others are careful to protect our precious resources. Why some people lie, cheat and steal, while their own brother or sister – raised in the same manner in the same house by the same parents – are honest, straightforward and kind. Why must there be wars? We questioned whether there was a higher being, and if so and they were good, why would they allow so much evil in the world. We spoke of numerous things and pondered many of life's unanswered questions.

"Near the end of the third day, Asta invited me to meditate with him. We faced each other and crossed our legs in the lotus position. I closed my eyes, and as I had learned to do, cleared my mind of all thoughts and ideas. It was as if a heavy summer rain had washed everything from my mind and left an unspoiled, mirror-like lake. I fell deeper and deeper into my meditation until I was no longer aware of my body. I was floating in a void and I could feel Asta's spirit within me. His spirit led me on a journey that included visions of jungles, witch doctors, camels, worms, castles, firecrackers and much more. It was a unusual journey that revealed me hugging very sick children, sticking needles in old men and eating sweets with a Chinese emperor. When the meditation ended, Asta placed a map into my hands.

"'Go on this journey, Mateo. Follow this map and find answers to the questions we have pondered. With those answers perhaps you can help save our troubled world.'

"'I am too old," I replied, "and too frail for such a difficult journey.'

"Asta looked deep into my eyes and said, 'Give it to your son, he will do it.'

"Since I had never married and had no children, I was confused by his message. But as I looked up from the map to explain that to Asta, he was gone. He had disappeared. Gone also were his heavily muscled young men, his flowers and his mat. One moment he was sitting directly across from me, holding my hand, and in the next moment, he and his troupe had vanished.

"I waded back to the Ganges' shore and left India the very next day. After months of hard travel, I came home to my native Spain to die. Ricardo, then you found me," concluded the señor.

Señor Vasquez looked affectionately at Ricardo. "I had no one. You and your family showed me love and respect. I wish to repay you."

From under his shirt, the Señor pulled out a shriveled, rolled up animal skin. He unraveled it to reveal the map from his story.

"Ricardo, this is all I have of value. I give it to you now, as if you were my son. This is your inheritance from me. I want you to see the wonders of the world as I did. If you follow this map, you will visit many fascinating places and meet many interesting people. As you discover the world, you will discover much about yourself as well.

"My hope for you is that as you travel, you will experience the thrill of unusual adventures, the joy of new friends and the amazement of embracing different cultures. May you also experience the beauty of returning home to those you love."

Señor Vasquez, with the pride of a diamond cutter who was holding his most perfectly cut stone, handed it to Ricardo. Señor Vasquez hugged the boy, and whispered fiercely in his ear, "Follow the map, Ricardo. As you do, may you learn that by your courage and your actions, you can help those who are less fortunate than you. You can make a difference in the lives of those who are in need and at risk. You can help change our world, Ricardo."

The two walked back into the apartment, where they found Alberto, Marta, Anna and Esteban nervously anticipating Ricardo's farewell. Ricardo held his brother and sister close and made them promise to always watch over each other.

Marta handed Ricardo his pack and jacket and told him there was a note in a hidden pocket she sewed into the jacket lining. They embraced, tears flowing like an early March melt in the mountains.

"I love you, Mother."

Marta simply could not speak, but squeezed her son tightly.

Ricardo then knelt beside his father who was sobbing uncontrollably. Alberto was always sensitive about his children, but his weakened condition made him even more emotional than usual.

"Father, don't worry about me. I am strong and resourceful. I will remember everything that you and Mother have taught me."

Fighting back tears, Ricardo continued, "Promise me you will get well soon. I will be home before you know it."

Alberto pulled his son to him and through his tears he managed to say, "I love you, Ricardo. I always will. You are my heart. May God be with you."

With trembling hands, Alberto handed his son a package.

Ricardo stood as straight as a soldier on parade, slipped his pack over his shoulders, and grabbed his jacket, the package, and the map. He took a tearful last look at his beloved family, then at Señor Vasquez. Ricardo turned and walked briskly out the door. He never looked back, not even once.

Chapter Four
The Aviela

sing the name from his map, Ricardo said to the captain, "I want to sail to the *Dark Continent*."

"To Africa, you mean, lad," the captain replied in a raspy voice. He was a burly, red-faced man with a bushy white beard. His eyes bulged a little, and upon a closer look, Ricardo could see many broken blood vessels on his face, like the face of a heavy drinker.

"That will cost you 400 pesos."

"I have little money. Is there a cheaper way?"

"For 200 pesos, you can bring your own food and sleep on the deck."

"May I work for my passage, sir?" Ricardo asked politely.

"Yes, you may," the captain answered, mocking Ricardo's proper use of the word. "You may swab the decks during the day. You may wash the dishes at night. You may sleep on the deck, and you may eat the crew's leftovers, if there are any."

"I'll do it, sir."

"What is your name, lad?"

"Ricardo. Ricardo Columbo, sir."

"We sail first thing in the morning; don't be late. By the way, if anyone asks, you have NO money, not little money as you said before. These scoundrels will kill you for your 'little' money. Do you understand, Ricardo Columbo?"

"Yes, Captain. I'll be here first thing in the morning. And thank you, sir."

Ricardo walked down the gangplank. Fearing he might be late for the early morning sail, he found a spot on the pier between some of the huge ropes that held the *Aviela*. He took some bread and jelly from his sack and ate hungrily. The ropes whined and moaned as each wave reached the shore, like carriers struggling under the weight of a large Indian maharaja. That vision made Ricardo smile as he closed his eyes and fell into a deep sleep.

He woke the next morning to the sound of hundreds of screeching gulls as they dove for their breakfast and fought over their catch. Ricardo felt the ropes move quickly beneath him. The Aviela was moving without him! He followed the moving rope until it neared the end of the pier. "Well, here goes my first real adventure," he thought as he grabbed onto the anaconda-like rope, slipped it between his back and his pack and held on for his life. The rope moved faster and faster as it was wound onto its winch, until it splashed heavily into the water.

Ricardo held his breath for longer than he thought possible. Every time the rope whipped him out of the water, he took a huge gasp of air, preparing himself for the next dunking. Ricardo was determined to get on board the ship. He saw the Aviela right in front of him through the ocean spray.

Just a moment longer, he thought, as he held his breath one last time.

Ricardo woke up on the deck of the Aviela with several crewmembers looking down at him. He gagged, rolled over and threw up a mixture of saltwater and the previous night's bread and jelly. Ricardo stuck his fingers in his mouth and gingerly pulled out strings of seaweed.

One of the blurry figures above him hissed, "I told you we were sailing first thing in the morning."

It was the captain, whose scowl quickly changed into a smile as he growled, "I admire your courage, Ricardo Columbo."

The captain was true to his word about Ricardo's routine aboard the Aviela. He swabbed the decks daily, and he washed dishes every night. But the captain found him a hammock below deck and introduced him to Carlo, the ship's cook. Carlo was from Marbello, a town on the southern coast of Spain with pristine beaches. According to Carlo. the sand was smooth, the salt water refreshing and the air – the air was simply exhilarating! It was the perfect place to heal body or mind. For years, Marbello had been known for its hospital, run by monks from the local monastery, and people travelled from all over Europe to be cured of illnesses like skin diseases and consumption. Carlo told Ricardo that he recalled seeing people come into his town with terribly flaking and itching skin, then leaving a month or two later with skin as soft as silk. The townspeople claimed the combination of the sun and the saltwater mist softened and healed the skin. The patients often considered this a miracle.

Eventually, so many travelers came to his town that the merchants, restaurant owners, innkeepers, and those who catered to the tourists raised their prices. They raised them year after year, and still people continued to visit. Except over time, Carlo recounted, the only people who came were those who could afford the high prices. This was especially true in the winter, when Marbella became a retreat for the continent's rich and famous.

Carlo's father, Pablo, had been head chef to such a family, the Van Dammes from Brussels, Belgium. The family visited Marbella every year before Europe's chilling winter set in, and stayed until the end of Lent. So from November to March, Pablo was busy planning, shopping, cooking, baking, decorating and supervising nightly banquets for the Van Dammes and their guests.

Meals were not just meals to the Van Dammes, but their reason to exist! The family made its living as traders and traveled all over the world buying goods to bring back and sell in Belgium, France, Holland, Spain and Portugal. On their business travels, they searched for the finest delicacies from every corner of the world. While purchasing silks from China, they ate *thousand-year-old eggs*. When they were scouting spices from Burma and India, they collected the recipe for *kao rou barbeque*, and when they contracted for hardwoods from Ceylon to be used in the finest cathedrals in Europe, they discovered *kutt hu roti*, deep-fried doughy pancakes with shredded beef. The more they traveled, the more exotic their tastes became. To Pablo, these foods were downright strange.

The Van Dammes fancied peacock, pheasant, llama, puffin hearts and mountain goat, and almost any dish cooked in cream or butter. There was *escamole* made from ant larvae, *eri polu* made with silkworm pupa, and *phan pyut*, a dish of rotted potatoes treated with spices. That dish could be served with venomous snake wine. Every meal included cheeses, nuts and fruits, mountains of fresh-baked rolls and bread, and, of course, scrumptious desserts. There was *stargazey pie* with fish heads poking up through the piecrust, and roasted pears with mascarpone cream. Elise, their eight year old daughter, developed a taste for *sugar plums* and *currant tarts*. It was all delicious and irresistible to the family. It was also very fattening and unhealthy.

No matter how he tried, and no matter how many times he baked or fried those delicacies, Pablo could not get used to the rich, exotic food. He was simply a meat, fish and potatoes lover. "Give me a loaf of peasant bread, some red wine, a little beef and potatoes, and I'm happy," he would tell Carlo. "Not this culinary circus!"

But Pablo had natural and creative skills, which the Van Dammes recognized. He also needed the income, which conveniently allowed him free time from April to October when he could fish, hike and spend time with his family.

Carlo loved fishing with his father. He enjoyed cleaning the snapper or redfish right off the side of their boat, then bringing the fish home to proudly show his mother. Pablo would then cook the fish, simply. Usually, he grilled it with some onions, but occasionally Pablo would coat the top of the fish with a heavy layer of salt so when it was baked, all the flavor remained sealed into the meat of the fish. No matter how Pablo prepared the fish, it was always simple and wonderful! Carlo often helped Pablo with the cooking and felt at ease in the kitchen. After all, he had been watching his father work since he was a baby. The kitchen floor was his play space; the cups, bowls and ladles were his toys.

One June day, when Carlo was twelve, he and Pablo concluded a successful day of fishing when they were caught in a sudden, violent storm. It was like an explosion! The waves pounded against their little boat over and over again, until Pablo took off his belt and used it to strap Carlo to the top of an empty cask. He placed a goatskin filled with their fresh water around Carlo's neck. "If we turn over, stay on this cask – no matter what," he told Carlo. Moments later, a giant wave crashed into them, breaking their boat into pieces. Carlo and the cask were thrown into the water. Carlo searched for his father, using a broken plank for an oar. Sadly, he could not find him. Carlo called out for his father over and over again.

"Papa, Papa, it's Carlo! Answer me, Papa, please!"

Night came, and Carlo tried to convince himself that his father swam for help, so in the morning, he began searching again. Carlo was spotted by a ship of Her Majesty's Spanish Fleet and was rescued.

Carlo looked for his father in every seaport and fishing village, but never found him. After a week, he went home to his family. They were overjoyed to see Carlo, but devastated to learn about Pablo's fate. Carlo's mother was so saddened by the loss of her husband that she rarely spoke again. Carlo raised his brothers until they were in their teens, and then he headed out to sea.

It was only natural for Carlo to become a ship's cook.

He cooked in the style of his father by offering simple yet healthy fare, which the crew appreciated. After a long, tiring day in the burning sun, they were treated to cold *gazpacho* soup, or after a battle with a wet rain, he cooked them comfort food like meat and potatoes or pasta. Not once did he cook or bake in the style of the Van Dammes. Every meal's simplicity was in honor of his father and what he learned from him.

Carlo had never told any of his shipmates about losing his father to the sea, but every morning after he made the crew breakfast, and every evening after dinner, he would walk up and down the deck of the Aviela, near the rail, and look down at the water. It was an impossible fantasy that he might find his father floating on a log or swimming alongside the ship, yet he never stopped looking. Carlo kept to himself and never let anyone get close to him, especially the captain. Deep inside Carlo was afraid that he would be abandoned once again.

Surprisingly though, in just a few days, Carlo connected with Ricardo. He was captivated by Ricardo's willingness to learn and listen, his high energy, and his respectful manners. Ricardo was not sassy or rude like so many other boys the cook had encountered over the years. Carlo asked Ricardo if he would like to learn to cook, and to be his apprentice. So, with the captain's approval, Carlo began teaching Ricardo to chop, cut and slice potatoes. Then, he showed him how to sauté onions, cayenne peppers, garlic, tomatoes and paprika, and to place the mixture on fresh-sliced bread and bake it a few minutes in the oven. Ricardo was a quick study. He learned how to slice beef with the grain so it wasn't stringy, and how to make pasta noodles, pulling them by hand until they were thin and ready to cook with a little olive oil. Carlo taught Ricardo how to bake bread so the crust was hard and the center was soft, and how to make the most out of very few ingredients.

Ricardo felt at home on the Aviela, especially in the kitchen with Carlo, but at night when he lay in his hammock, he would think about his real home, his mother and father, Esteban, Anna and Señor Vasquez. He recited a nightly prayer for each of them, trying to picture his loved ones in his mind, but he rarely got through them all before sleep overtook his weary body.

North Africa was only a short sail from southern Spain, but the Aviela had several scheduled stops to make along the western coast before it reached its final destination in Guinea, the first place marked on Ricardo's map. Once there, the Avelia would unload its cargo of cloth and perfumes and exchange them for a most precious commodity: salt. The captain and Carlo were both pleased that their young helper would accompany them. Somehow, Ricardo's presence brought the captain and the cook closer together.

One day, Ricardo began telling them about his mother's Friday night dinners. That led the captain to share memories of his own mother's stew, which in turn inspired Carlo to prepare a stew for the three of them that very night. The stew was delicious. Carlo and the captain each had three servings, and with the help of a glass of wine accompanying each portion, they began to tell stories about their childhoods.

The lively conversation continued among the three of

them for several nights over dinner, and they spoke late into the night.

On the third night, after a meal of *paella*, fresh bread and wine, Carlo, almost in a whisper, told his story about his father. He told them about the storm, his search, his mother and brothers, every little detail. Tears welled up in his eyes, but he fought back his need to cry. He sniffed a bit and just then, the captain reached over and gently put his big hand on Carlo's shoulder and pulled him closer. Without any hesitation, Carlo put his head in the crook of the captain's arm and sobbed.

For what seemed like a very long time, the captain held him. Neither the captain nor Ricardo said a word. When Carlo finally lifted his head from the captain's arm, he used his shirt to wipe his face and dry his eyes, and Ricardo noticed that Carlo looked different! He looked younger and calmer, as if a huge burden had been lifted from him. Ricardo was pleased he had been a part of Carlo's journey. He also realized it had been more than twenty years since Carlo had a friend – and now the captain would be his friend for life.

Chapter Five
Father's Gift

icardo kept the farewell package his father had given him strapped to his backpack. For many days, he looked at it and touched it, but left it unopened. It was as though opening the package would finalize his separation from his family, in particular his father, and Ricardo was not ready for that.

Finally, late one night in his hammock, Ricardo untied the leather straps, unfolded the oilcloth wrap, and gazed upon its contents. He smiled. Inside were more than thirty separate packages: fourteen bottles and eighteen jars, all carefully labeled in his father's handwriting. There was also a small mortar and pestle.

Ricardo picked up one of the packages and read: *sweet weeds, Althea: for sore throat and cough, as a tea.* The second package was labeled *king of bitters: topically for snakebite, a tea for flu and fever,* and the next package read *elephant gall or aloe: apply to burns, frostbite, orally as a laxative.* Ricardo handled each piece and read every label carefully.

His father had made him a portable pharmacist's kit; what a wonderful and useful gift! Ricardo was touched by his father's thoughtfulness and tried to imagine the effort it took his sick and weakened father to assemble this kit. He rewrapped the packages and held it up to his nose, trying to capture a trace of his father's scent, but all he could smell was the oilcloth, the herbs and the sea. Ricardo placed the package next to his right cheek and slowly rubbed it against his skin, thinking about how much he loved his father and how his father must love him. He fell asleep that night with the package as his pillow.

When he awakened, Ricardo reopened the pouch and re-read each individual label. *Black walnut hulls, mix with garlic. Add three drops of lavender oil; apply to burning & itching feet.*

Follow with powder of green clay and lavender to keep feet dry.

He searched the vials and located the bottle of *lavender oil* and then the jar of *green clay.*

Valerian, make tea for sleeplessness, put a drop of lavender oil under pillow as well.

Catnip for fever, add peppermint drops for taste. Ricardo didn't realize that catnip had uses other than pleasing cats, and for a moment he thought of his own cat, Midnight, who would curl next to him at night, purring with contentment.

Among the items Ricardo's father had provided was a small gray notebook filled with medical and pharmacy facts, written in the tiniest printed letters.

Gas: chew fennel seeds after meals, will also freshen breath. One can also drink peppermint and chamomile tea. Eye Problems: slice cucumber, softens tissues around eye. Black tea, tannins draw out excess fluids. Use cold compress, do not touch or rub eye.

Nausea: crackers, ginger and peppermint

Toothache: Crush anise seeds, apply directly

Ricardo was fascinated by how many times *apple cider*

vinegar was mentioned in the little grey journal. Surprisingly, it could *heal bites, indigestion, heat stroke, and even urinary tract infections, when combined with cranberry juice.*

There was also a bottle with a dropper labeled *Alberto's secret formula for extreme pain, anxiety and anger. Use only two drops for adults, one drop for children. Very potent.*

Just as Ricardo was reassembling his kit, he heard a loud shriek coming from the kitchen. He jumped down from his bunk and ran to find Mia, a sailor from Portugal, bent over in pain, holding his left hand. "Help me! Please help me! I burned my hand on the stove!" Ricardo swiftly turned, ran to his bunk, and returned with his kit.

He tried to calm Mia, convincing him to hold out his hand. First, Ricardo placed it in a bucket of cool water to speed healing and ease the pain, as he had learned from his father. He was careful not to break the skin as he applied a few drops of lavender and chamomile oils. All the while, Ricardo was softly, yet confidently speaking. "It will be fine, Mia. Breathe deeply, Mia." Ricardo took out the package marked *aloe*, opened it, and picked up a single leaf.

He tore the leaf apart lengthwise and squeezed out a sticky, cool gel onto the burn. Mia relaxed! Ricardo removed his shirt, tore off a piece, and then tore that piece into strips about three fingers wide to wrap Mia's hand and keep the aloe in place. "We'll change this dressing twice more today and once again in the morning," Ricardo reassured Mia. "Keep it dry and elevated to keep the swelling down."

Several of the crew had come running when they heard Mia's screams and watched as Ricardo tended to his burns. "Nice work, Ricardo," said Miguel, a helmsman from Valencia. "A real doctor, you are. You can take care of me any time."

Mia said, "Thanks, Ricardo. I was reaching into the pot for a piece of ham when the ship suddenly rocked and I grabbed the pot for balance. That really, really hurt!"

Ricardo changed Mia's dressing in the afternoon and again that night, each time dropping on lavender and chamomile oils and applying aloe gel. When Ricardo unwrapped Mia's hand the next morning, the swelling had subsided but it was still a bit red, but not bright red.

That day, Ricardo was a hero. Even the captain complimented him on his efforts. The crew stopped calling him Ricardo, and instead they nicknamed him "Doc." Ricardo liked that name, and in his prayers that night, he thanked his father and Señor Bracco for their pharmacy lessons. "Doctor Columbo sounds very agreeable," Ricardo thought as he closed his eyes.

Chapter Six
A Dream of Nana

hat very night, Ricardo had a dream about his grandmother. She was called Nana by her three grandchildren, and although she died when Ricardo was a young boy, he still had a very clear picture of her in his mind. He could see her wearing her light pink nightshirt with her matching pink slippers standing in front of her apartment in Madrid. Ricardo loved his nana and still missed her very much. She made him feel safe and loved, and she regaled him with stories about her childhood, her parents and how things were in the "olden days." He especially enjoyed Nana's stories about her daughter, his mother,

Marta. Nana could recall his mother's birth, schooling, friends and experiences down to the tiniest detail.

"Once, when your mother was about six years old, she was in a dancing show, dressed in a yellow costume. Your grandfather moved close to the stage to get a better view of his daughter. She spotted him, and as the other eleven girls continued their dance routine, Marta stopped dancing, smiled broadly and called out, 'Hola, Papa.' It was very sweet. She was very sweet!"

Another story that Ricardo liked was when his Marta was four years old and playing princess with Nana. "I am the princess and you love me, please act as though you love me," Marta said.

So Nana hugged her and told her she loved her.

"No, Mother, show me you really love me." So Nana squeezed Marta and said over and over again how much she loved her little princess.

"No, Mother, I mean you should really, really, really show me how much you love me."

"Darling Marta, I don't know what else I can do to show

you how much I love you. What do you want me to do?"

And Ricardo's mother replied, perhaps thinking of a picture she had seen or perhaps a vision of love she had, "I want to see those love hearts in your eyes!"

It was hard to imagine his mother at the age of four, or being so very innocent, but when Nana shared that story with her eyes sparkling and her soft laughter, Ricardo felt content.

Now, as Ricardo slept, his nana came to him. She was on her balcony, waiting for her three treasured grandchildren to visit. She waved happily when she saw them coming up the street, and they waved back and started to run toward her.

Just then, from behind a large oak, out jumped two terrible looking men wearing black leather pants and boots. Their shirts, gloves and the masks over their eyes were also a deep black. The children immediately sensed danger, and Anna and Esteban moved back toward Ricardo.

"Well, what do we have we here?" asked the taller of the two men. "Three little prizes for our auction. You will each bring a small fortune at the slave market in Casablanca."

The two pulled out large nets from behind their backs and started chasing the children down the street. Ricardo yelled to the children, "Run to Nana's!" and bravely turned to face the devils in black. A net dropped over his head, and within seconds Ricardo was captured. They bound his feet and hands with rope and left him to lie there while they chased after the younger children. One grabbed Anna by the wrist, and the other had thrown Esteban, kicking and screaming, over his shoulders. Both were caught.

Suddenly, Nana appeared. She came in her usual nightshirt and slippers, but she also carried a sword and a shield. The shield had a six-pointed star on its face with a spike coming out of its center. She raised the sword, which glistened in the sunlight, and rushed the kidnappers. "Let my grandchildren go!"

The two intruders, amused by this little old lady in pink slippers challenging them, released the children. "Any other orders you'd like to give us before you die, granny?"

The taller man drew a six-inch dagger as the other man began swinging a metal chain with a weight on the end. He circled that chain over his head as he moved to Nana's left, and his partner slithered to her right. He let fly the weapon aimed at Nana's head. She sidestepped and took the blow with her shield. With the sword in her right hand, she lashed out and cut deeply into the hand holding the dagger.

The assailant screamed loudly as his dagger dropped to the ground with a thud. Nana turned and faced dagger man's partner, who was dumbfounded by Nana's skill with the weapons. He lunged at her for a moment, then turned and ran away. Perhaps he reconsidered when he saw the point of the spike so close to his face. The other man followed behind him. Anna and Esteban ran crying into Nana's arms, and with a graceful motion, Nana cut Ricardo free, then dropped her sword and shield.

The three children looked in amazement at their nana. She smiled at them and said, "In family, there is strength."

When Ricardo woke, he pondered what that dream might mean. He thought about how Nana died. She was a week shy of her 92nd birthday, when she slipped in her kitchen and hit her head on the floor.

The doctor told the family that at her age and weakened condition, she would only last a few short hours. The family gathered. Nana lay quietly in her bed, as her children and grandchildren stayed by her side. One by one, they whispered quietly in her ears, and told her how much she meant to them and how they would never forget her.

On Friday evening, with Nana slipping in and out of consciousness, the family lit candles in her room, sang songs and told her stories with the hope that she could somehow hear them. This was a sad but tender memory for Ricardo. His nana lay dying, but her room, like her life, was filled with family and with love.

As Nana closed her eyes for the last time, Ricardo knew at that moment, just like he knew now, that Nana would always be with him. It was not just because her blood ran through his veins; it was because her spirit lived in him. He truly missed his nana, with her soft skin, loving smile, and her pink nightshirt and slippers.

Chapter Seven
Farewell Dinner

he Aviela's voyage ended in the early evening in West Africa in the port of Kamsar, Guinea, by the mouth of the Rio Nunez River. This spot was quite near the first X on the map Señor Vasquez had given to Ricardo. The captain and crew wanted to say farewell to Ricardo with food and drinks at a local pub on the waterfront. They would enjoy one night of beer and frivolity with their young companion, then catch a few hours rest before restocking their provisions in the morning and heading north for their return trip to Spain.

At the pub there was so much food – mostly pork, potatoes and beans. In accordance with his family's traditions,

Ricardo never touched the pork. He listened to speeches and toasts to "Doc" by Mia and others who Ricardo had helped heal during the voyage. Mia detailed the medical miracle Ricardo performed on his badly burned hand. Fredric talked about the splint Ricardo cleverly made for his broken wrist, that allowed him to continue his deckhand chores throughout the voyage. All agreed that, due to the solution of fennel and peppermint Ricardo encouraged them to drink each night before bedtime, they had less cramping and gas than ever before. Carlo praised Ricardo for quickly learning his way around the Aviela's galley and proclaimed that if Ricardo decided not to be a doctor, he could instead become a fine chef.

Out of the corner of his eye, Ricardo noticed two African men listening intently to the crew of the Aviela. They were tall and quite regal looking in their colorful tribal robes. They were obviously men of importance, since standing on guard only a few feet away were four young warriors whose eyes searched the room constantly, as if they were mother giraffes watching over their babies, on the lookout for hungry lions on the prowl.

The two leaders were following the stories and toasts quite intently, pausing only for an occasional sip on a beer or a bite from the rice and beans on the wooden plates in front of them.

When the captain spoke, the crew fell silent out of respect. He told Ricardo, "You will always have a place on the Aviela and in my heart." Some of the crew had been with the captain for years, and never before had they heard him speak in such a warm and fatherly manner. "I carved this for you," said the captain quietly as he handed Ricardo a small wooden spoon with a ship's anchor cut into its handle. A moment later, the captain returned to form, breaking up the party and informing the crew that they had a salt resupply day ahead, before embarking for Europe.

Many backslaps, handshakes and a few hugs later, Ricardo was alone, reflecting on the first leg of his journey and the many friends he had made. As always, during these quiet moments, he thought of his family.

When Ricardo woke up several hours later, he was

bound, gagged and strapped to the back of a donkey on a deeply rutted road.

AFRICA

Chapter Eight
The Jungle

icardo's head was spinning and he was on the verge of vomiting from the donkey ride when the motion suddenly stopped.

"What has happened to me?" wondered Ricardo. "Did I fall and hit my head after I said goodbye to the crew? Why am I tied to the back of this animal which, by the way, smells really awful?"

He was gently lifted off the donkey and laid down on a carpet, he heard someone giving orders in strange tongue. His ties were loosened and the gag removed, and it took a few moments for his eyes to adjust to the light. Ricardo looked into a room full of men dressed in red robes flowing to the ground. They sat in a semicircle around their chief, whose robe had royal blue trim at the cuffs while the bottom hem was the same color red as his tribesmen.

The chief, a handsome and powerfully built man, was staring into Ricardo's eyes. He spoke perfect Catalan Spanish, and was obviously quite well educated.

"Welcome to our village, I am Hin, the tribal chief. I apologize for the manner in which we brought you here, but my warriors were afraid you would not accept a polite invitation to join us in the jungle to help us with our medical problem, Doctor."

"Doctor?" thought Ricardo. 'They have me confused with someone else."

"Water, please," were the first words out of Ricardo's parched lips. A bowl of cool, fresh water immediately appeared before him. He gulped it down, tried to compose himself by taking a few slow deep breaths, and then spoke.

"My name is Ricardo Columbo from Madrid, Spain. My father is Alberto Columbo, a pharmacist. My mother is Marta Columbo, a teacher of classical languages. I came here as a cabin boy yesterday on the ship Aviela. I am only 14 years old and am certainly not a doctor!"

"My warriors heard your friends speak of your great medical feats and how you helped them when they were hurt and sick. How do you explain that, if you are not a doctor?"

At that moment, Ricardo wondered how a tribal chief in West Africa learned to speak European languages with such great ease and comfort as if he was born in Spain.

Without waiting for Ricardo's reply to his question, the chief explained.

"We had a Catholic priest living in our village for many years. He was a linguist. He taught our royal family how to read and converse in Spanish, Latin and Hebrew, as well as in our native tongue. He was like a second father to me, a brother to my late father, King Zet. His passing was a great loss to our tribe and to me personally."

"How did you know what I was thinking that very instant?" asked Ricardo.

"Our tribe has a skill passed down through many generations. We are mind readers – or more accurately, we are trained to anticipate thoughts and questions based on particular circumstances. It drives the people outside of our tribe absolutely crazy! We can go into that further at another time, Ricardo Columbo. Why do they call you 'doctor' and talk of your healing skills?"

Ricardo recounted to the chief his experiences collecting medicinal plants with his father, his apprenticeship with Señor Bracco, and his work helping patients at the La Latina Hospital, emptying their bedpans and controlling their fevers during the plague. He explained to the chief that, while some people that he helped thought he had a gift for healing, and perhaps he did, he was a long way from actually being a doctor of medicine.

"My son, Armoldo, has an affliction. I don't call it a disease – it is more of a curse! I had hoped you could help him. Would you see if your healing 'gift' might help my son?"

In the rear of the village, in a hut made of mud, sticks and palm leaves, lay Armoldo. He was barely five years old and his body was twisted and knotted. Somehow, he reminded Ricardo of the pretzels they sold on the streets back home in Madrid. Armoldo had huge, sad eyes and was in obvious pain. When you looked at him from a few feet away, it seemed like all you could see of his face were his piercing eyes. At first, Armoldo would not look at Ricardo.

But instead of recoiling or pulling back from his disfigurement as many faith healers and witch doctors had done since Armoldo was born, Ricardo reached out and tenderly stroked Armoldo's face. He put his head next to Armoldo's, their foreheads touching. A slight smile came to Armoldo's lips, his eyes lightened just a bit. Later when the chief recalled that first meeting, he would say, "Armoldo 's first smile in years made the hut literally glow with light."

When Ricardo tried to move the young boy's twisted arm, then his gnarled leg, Armoldo screamed in pain. His agonized howls were heard throughout the village. Because of that, Ricardo was viewed with superstition and, in some cases, with hostility by the tribe. The head healer and witch doctor, Olin, helped fan these feelings by speaking of 'the outsider's poison,' and claiming that Armoldo's screams were pleas to stop this torture."

Ricardo immediately realized that he must somehow get Olin to support his efforts to heal Armoldo– or at least not work against them. He asked the Chief to arrange a private meeting between him and Olin. At this meeting, Ricardo offered Olin some of *Alberto's Secret Formula*, just two drops on his tongue, and in a few minutes they were laughing and singing. Ricardo promised to teach the witch doctor about his herbs and ointments if Olin would teach him about the cures to be found in the jungle. Olin had many, since his father and grandfather before him had been tribal healers.

They had shown Olin how to use *honey* to take the pain out of a bee sting and to make a *mustard powder footbath* to lower a fever. He learned how to treat a snakebite, which was a constant threat in the jungle using a mixture of *coconut* and *tea tree oil,* while he calmed the victim with lavender oil and made him drink a potion of *turmeric* and *Echinacea root.*

Ricardo asked if he could assist Olin in his efforts to heal Armoldo. Olin accepted his help, no longer feeling that his position as tribal healer was threatened.

Ricardo asked to have his things brought to him, and

soon he was searching through the medical pack his father gave to him and paging through his notes.

Arnica for muscle cramps…shake well and rub into muscle

Chamomile and peppermint oils…massage into sore muscle

For anxiety and relaxation…feverfew and saffron flowers, grind together with chamomile, soak overnight and make tea. Place lavender behind patient's ears for calming effect.

Remember the value of deep tissue massage, stretching and targeted muscle release.

Ricardo had seen how the nurses at La Latina Hospital stretched and massaged their patients' aching muscles, sometimes for hours at a time. For those patients who could afford it, private nurses continued the therapy for days and even weeks on end. They were happy to show Ricardo the pressure points and benefits of massage, and let him work with their patients from time to time.

He had also spent several days with Ramon, the hospital "bone adjuster."

Ramon seemed to work miracles by snapping a twisted neck or an out-of-joint backbone into place, and by putting intense pressure on one small spot on a muscle. He called it *active release*, where a painful tight muscle freed itself because of the pressure being applied to it.

Ricardo had helped Ramon by pulling down on the pelvis and hips of a victim of a cart accident while Ramon gently pushed his backbones until they heard a click. The man literally jumped off the table and kissed Ramon. He was pain free!

Ricardo suggested they begin gently massaging Armoldo's muscles with the oils, not just for an hour or two, but all day and all night, even while he slept. They asked the chief to select an honor guard, who they would train to become experts in stretching and massage.

Because the work on Armoldo was initially so painful, especially the stretching, Ricardo gave him a drop of *Alberto's Secret Formula* every four hours to relieve him. Over time, the drops were given every eight hours, then just at bedtime, and then, thankfully, not at all.

Ricardo asked Olin to give Armoldo an orphaned monkey that was born just two days earlier near the village. The boy rarely let the monkey out of his sight, and as Ricardo had suggested, Armoldo held onto, and sang to his pet whenever the muscle pain became unbearable. The tune Ricardo taught Armoldo to sing was from an old nursery rhyme his mother used to sing to him at bedtime: *Asserrin, Asserran.* The song went like this:

I am Armoldo, son of Hin

My strength is deep, it comes from within,

It comes from my ancestors, our search to be free

Pain is no stranger to them or to me,

I will fight this condition, and I will be

As straight and as tall as a date palm tree,

My name is Armoldo, son of Hin

My strength is deep, it comes from within.

With each passing day, Armoldo's muscles relaxed and were a bit more elongated. After a month, he could open his clenched fist, and after two months, he was able to raise his arms over his head. In just four months, he could actually stand. He was bent over, but he was standing.

Remembering his days with Ramon, Ricardo asked the

Royal Guard to add pulling and lengthening Armoldo's entire body to their daily routine. Two guards would get behind Armoldo and pull on his neck, and two more guards would stand at his feet and gently pull at the same time.

One day, when Ricardo and Olin were watching Armoldo being stretched out as far as it seemed he could possibly go, Ricardo jumped onto the boy's back and pushed down on his back bone. Everyone in the hut heard the huge click.

Armoldo warily came off the ground and rose to his hands and knees. Then he stood up as straight as the African palm he had been singing about. He walked over and hugged Ricardo and Olin. Hin called for a huge tribal feast that night in celebration. There was dancing around a campfire and servings of roasted wild boar, *poulet yassa* (a succulent chicken dish with lemon and onions) and *tigadegena* (peanut stew). The children loved the *meni-meniyong* (a sweet made with honey and sesame) and *baobob* (fruit dipped in carob syrup).

Every day after that, the chief and his son would walk

through the village to cheers of jubilation. Ricardo would join in some of those walks, and it was then that the chief would teach him how to "read minds."

Armoldo was not the only body that was changing during this time. Ricardo too, looked different. He was nearly fifteen years old now and was developing hair under his arms and some peach fuzz on his face and chest. He was becoming quite strong and muscular.

Ricardo began to spend time with the tribal warriors. At first, they just talked and learned to communicate with each other, then they wrestled for fun, then Ricardo was invited to train with the warriors. Over his several months in the village, he became proficient with the bow and arrow, spear and knife throwing, tracking, survival skills, and more. The warriors were physically very fit. They were able to lift boulders, climb trees, swing on vines and run like the wind, and Ricardo was right there beside them.

Ricardo became an honorary member of the tribe and of the royal family.

"Anything you wish, Ricardo. Simply ask and it is

yours," said the chief. "I offer you twenty head of cattle, a hut with a view of the river, even my daughter Ada's hand in marriage."

"I am honored by your generosity and affection, Chief. All I truly wish for, along with your family's good health and happiness, is to continue my journey. I have many more adventures ahead of me, and I am ready to see what is behind the next mountain or river bend."

So with drums beating, twelve of the tribe's strongest warriors escorted Ricardo out of the village. Ricardo said goodbye to Olin, to Hin and, most lovingly, to Armoldo. Goodbyes are often sad, but Ricardo knew it was time.

Chapter Nine
Ride With the Warriors

he warriors accompanied Ricardo on the tribe's best horses. Shortly after they left the village, Ricardo felt a bulge in his right pocket. He was worried that a strange creature from the jungle had crawled inside his clothes. He carefully reached in his pocket and pulled out a glorious diamond that the chief had hidden there while they hugged goodbye. He remembered the chief whispering to him, "May this guide you on your quest." Ricardo had wondered what he meant at the time. He moved the diamond to the secret pocket of his jacket.

The warriors followed along a worn path to the east, and

Ricardo saw baboons, hyenas, wild boar and antelope in the jungle as they rode, as well as crocodiles whenever they neared the river. All of this fascinated Ricardo – all except the many snakes they saw. There were vipers, cobras, and the scariest of all, black mambas! Ricardo really disliked snakes. They frightened him and gave him a cold chill up his spine. Once, Ricardo saw four dogs trap a twenty-foot-long black mamba against a tree. The dogs were barking excitedly at the snake, which was coiled and ready to strike. In an instant, the barking stopped, all was quiet and the snake slithered away. Ricardo learned one of the lessons of the jungle that day. Most African snakes are dangerous, but mambas are deadly!

Many times during the ride east, Ricardo reached into his hidden pocket to make certain the diamond was still there. One of those times, he found the eighteen pesos carefully wrapped in this note:

Dear Ricardo,

May God watch over you and protect you. May you come home to us safely and very soon. We love you. חי

Mother, Father, Anna and Esteban

Ricardo did not know what the symbol that looked like a camel was, but he imagined it was some sort of good luck sign.

After ten days, Ricardo and his warrior escorts arrived at the oasis town of Timbuktu in Mali, the second spot on his map, where they encountered a caravan of travelers.

The warriors paid the caravan master handsomely to take special care of Ricardo. "If anything happens to this boy, we will track you down and you will pay with your life." Ali, the caravan master, promised to give Ricardo his best camel and to treat him with great care.

Ricardo asked Ali, "Where is your caravan going?"

He replied excitedly, "We are going to the center of the world and the home of the Jews. We are going to Jerusalem, my son."

Chapter Ten
Timbuktu

imbuktu was a lush oasis town filled with beautiful gardens. It was also marked on Ricardo's map. The Niger River ran alongside the town, and by building canals and a series of small dams, the farmers were able to grow lemon trees, date palms and acres of beautiful flowers. They called Timbuktu *The Pearl of the Desert*.

The area around Timbuktu was a fertile savannah, a place where wealthy and educated families from Arab and African countries would spend their summers. Along the banks of the river, people from the Arab north and the African south merged, grew to know and, sometimes, respect and enjoy each other's food, arts and culture. Because of its location, Timbuktu was an active trading center where gold, diamonds, ivory, cereal and salt from the heart of Africa were bartered for silks from the Far East, cloth from India, jewelry from the Middle East, and perfumes from France.

There was also an active book trade, where the educated learned about the rest of the world's inventions, philosophies and religions. It was a scholarly melting pot.

Sadly, slaves were freely traded throughout the Arab and African world. Timbuktu was one of Africa's major slave trading centers.

The caravan master's full name was Ali ibn Nnamdi ibn Zakee al-Okafor, which meant he was Ali the son of Abdullah, grandson of Zakee, from the tribe of Okafor. Ali was an elderly trader who had been in the family trading business since he was a young boy. He learned the routes from the Atlantic Ocean across the Sahara Desert to Jerusalem from his father, who learned them from his father before him. The family had been trading goods from the jungles, such as kola nuts, ivory, and gold for more than fifty years. They also traded slaves. The family was wealthy, educated and very pleased with their station in life. Ricardo and Ali immediately bonded, not only because of the oath Ali swore to watch over his charge, but because they were both intelligent, curious and kind.

Ali gave Ricardo a camel named Kelen, which means "number one" in Arabic. Ali said Kelen was the pick of the herd when he was born. Ricardo soon learned that most camels have minds of their own, can be stubborn, and may even bite their owners. Kelen was different. From the minute Ricardo looked deep into his eyes, with their long double layer of eyelashes, Kelen was always even-tempered and co-operative. Ricardo and Kelen seemed to have an understanding that they were there to take care of each other.

Ricardo spent hours cleaning sand and dirt from Kelen's coat, removing tiny stones from his hooves and massaging his legs after a long days' march in the desert. Kelen basked in the attention and loved Ricardo as only an animal can love a person, completely and without reservation.

While Ricardo felt that Ali was a good man, he was confused and upset by something that happened the very first day they met. When Ali proudly gave Kelen to Ricardo, he also presented him with Martim, a twelve-year-old boy. Martim was a slave.

At first, Ricardo did not understand what Ali meant when he said, "Martim now belongs to you, Ricardo. He is my gift to you!"

Ricardo looked at Martim and back at Ali. "How can you give a person to another person? How can you give this boy to me? You do not own him, Ali."

"But I do. I do own him. He belongs to me!"

Ali explained to Ricardo that slave trading had existed in Africa for hundreds of years. Slaves were used as servants, soldiers, laborers, farmers and concubines.

Slave traders like Ali and his family would trade jewelry, cloth and silks for the slaves, then take them, along with gold, diamonds, ivory and other treasures from the jungle across the Sahara to the markets in Marrakesh, Cairo and Tunis. They would sell them at great profit to Arab and Berber princes, to wealthy Indian and Chinese families, or to anyone who was the highest bidder at the market.

"Where do the slaves come from?" Ricardo asked angrily.

"They are captives from warfare, from rivalries between tribes or clans, from conquests of neighboring kingdoms. The victors take the vanquished. It is as simple as that, Ricardo. They kill most of the warriors and capture the women and children to sell as slaves," Ali replied.

"The *Mandinke, Peul, Siongai, and Bambara* all have been enslaved by others, like my tribe, the *Dyula*. It is the way of our continent."

"It is cruel and inhuman," Ricardo cried out. "It is simply wrong."

Chapter Eleven
The Dyula

li explained to Ricardo that the Dyula lived in clans in villages across Mali. They taught their children the value of obedience, honesty, education and dedication to the Dyula people. There was great loyalty to the clan; inheritance went from father to son. The men were allowed to have multiple wives and were encouraged to marry within their own clan – in fact, cousins were preferred.

The Dyula taught their children about the *Great Mali Empire, Manden*. It was ruled by *Mansa Musa*, a former slave who became wealthy and expanded the empire by conquering Ghana and uniting hundreds of Mandinke clans across Central Africa.

There was a caste system in the empire. Near the top of the heap were the farmers who provided the nation with food. Then came the artisans, fishermen, scribes, civil servants, soldiers and, at the bottom, were the slaves.

Above them all were the wealthy and powerful traders who lived at the cultural crossroads of Africa and controlled the trade routes to the Middle East and to Europe.

Ali proudly told Ricardo, "We are Dyula, primarily gold traders. We treat our slaves much better here in Timbuktu than they do in the Arab North. The slaves we keep are in charge of our herds, our fields and our homes. They are our artisans, our entertainers and our children's nurses. We allow many of them to be educated and, in rare cases, to gain their freedom."

"But they are people, Ali!"

"They are, in fact, our merchandise, Ricardo!"

"I cannot accept this boy as my slave!"

Ali responded, "If you refuse him, he would simply be traded to a wealthy Arab, perhaps a cruel person at that. You will be helping Martim by allowing him to serve you. And you will need his help and experience along the journey across the desert."

Chapter Twelve
Martim

artim, who stood silently by during this conversation, faced Ricardo, put his hands in a prayer
pose in front of his heart, and said, "Please take
me, sir. I will work hard for you and will guard you with my
life!"

Ricardo wondered why Martim thought he would have
to guard him, but he agreed, saying, "You can join me as my
employee, even though I don't have much money to pay
you. I will not accept you as a slave, Martim. I would rather
you joined me as a friend."

"Then it's settled," said Ali. "Martim will teach you the

basics, like how to saddle and ride your camel, how to put up your tent during the hottest time of the day, how to prepare the food I'll give you, and much more."

The trip began with Ricardo learning how to ride Kelen. There is a certain rhythm to riding comfortably on a camel. For Ricardo, learning that rhythm included several days of extreme nausea.

For the first few days of his journey, each morning Ricardo reached into his father's pouch and ate ginger root to settle his stomach. By the end of the third day, Ricardo could ride Kelen without being sick or vomiting.

There was much to learn about camels. Also called "the ship of the desert," camel in Arabic means "beauty." Camels were first domesticated by the Berbers in the desert. It took forty days to cross the Sahara, and camels were the only animals capable of making that brutal crossing since they could travel for many days without food or water. Camels have a double row of eyelashes to block the sun and sand, and they can close their nostrils and ears to protect against blowing sand. Ricardo was stunned to learn that most caravans had

1,000 camels; and even one caravan was reported to stretch for many kilometers with more than 12,000 camels.

Ricardo learned that Martim was from Ghana, in Central Africa, not far from the Mali Empire where Timbuktu was located, and that he was a Mandinke.

One day, when Martim's father had been hunting in the jungle with the other warriors, one hundred Mali men raided their village. They easily overcame the elderly men who were standing guard, and took the women and children as captives – including Martim, who was only six years old!

Martim recalled with fear the noose they put around his neck and the long walk away from his home. He remembered watching the backs of his mother and his aunt, walking in front of the children, with their wrists tied and nooses around their necks. Together, they were part of a line of women, a few men, and many children who were all bound and terrified.

They walked for many days with little food or water until they arrived in Timbuktu, where they were sold to Ali and the other slave traders. Ali and his family kept Martim and his mother, MeMe, in their own house. MeMe became the head cook for the family, and Martim, being so young, started out as an errand boy.

Ali had quickly realized how smart Martim was and taught the boy how to read and write, to study numbers, mathematics and bookkeeping. At age twelve, Martim began to assist Ali with his business records and detail each transaction for gold, ivory or slaves.

Martim and MeMe were the lucky ones. Sadly, most of the others taken in the raid on their village were moved across the Sahara and sold into slavery. They were separated from their families, often beaten, and forced into a lifetime of despair.

There were others, mostly strong young men, who were sold to work in the salt mines. In the mines, the villagers were starved, beaten and brutalized. They were constantly abused, whipped to work faster and spent from early morning to late evening digging for salt. What a brutal life they led.

Chapter Thirteen
The Sahara

or the past 30 years, Ali had only hired Berber guides from the Azem family. The Azems knew the location of all the oases and how to navigate by the stars at night. With ties to their many Berber cousins, the Azem's travelling clients were protected from bandit raids during the long, difficult, forty-day trek in the desert. Unfortunately, the Azems were not available as guides this time, and Ali was a bit nervous. One of the Azem grandsons was marrying a cousin from a nearby tribe and the entire family was expected to attend. If the Azems did not show up, it would be considered a sign of disrespect.

The replacement guide was unknown to Ali. His name was Aksil Ben M'Hidi, and his father was distantly related to the Azem family. Aksil was tall, bearded and his eyes continually shifted away from Ali when they spoke.

As the journey began, with more than 1,000 camels tethered together in a line, there was excitement among the merchants and apprehension among the slaves. This was especially true for the young women, whose futures were most certainly bleak.

On the eighth day, as the caravan was bedding down after a meal, four Berber men in black robes silently crept into the camp and headed directly to Ricardo and Martim's tent.

One of the men cut the bottom of the tent with his saber, and the four jumped in and grabbed the boys. They pushed rags in the boys' mouths and tied their hands behind their backs with rope. Neither Ricardo or Martim had an opportunity to resist!

Two of the raiders lifted the boys onto camels, while their compatriots sat behind them, with knives pointed at

Ricardo and Martim's throats as they rode out into the desert blackness. The frightened boys did not know if this would be their last day alive!

Hours later in their Berber tent, the kidnappers laughed hysterically when they realized that Ricardo's camel, Kelen, had followed them out of the caravan camp. They congratulated themselves around a campfire. Although drinking alcohol was forbidden by their religion, they had quite a lot of it celebrating the capture of such a great prize as Ricardo.

"What a fine catch we have! A European doctor, his slave and his camel! Even when we give Aksil his share, we will earn a lot at the market. This package will bring us a huge price."

With his hands still tied behind him, Ricardo scooted along the blanket on his bottom until he reached the tent wall. He whistled and beat his hands against the bottom of the tent. Martim wondered what Ricardo was up to.

There was a ripping sound, and immediately Martim saw Kelen's nose, lips, teeth and then his entire head. Ricardo held up his hands and Kelen began to chew on the ropes until Ricardo's hands were free. Ricardo untied Martim and they crept through the hole in the tent.

As fate would have it, one of the Berber raiders decided to check on the captives at the same time. When he saw that Martim was untied and escaping, he grabbed him by his feet and held him tightly. Martim screamed, "Run Ricardo! Save yourself!"

Instead of running, Ricardo turned and grabbed the raider by the arm, and flipped him away from Martim, almost tearing the raider's arm from his shoulder. He had learned this move from his warrior friends in the jungle. The raider, with his arm hanging limply at his side, was still screaming in pain as Ricardo and Martim rode Kelen back to the safety of the caravan.

When they arrived, they found Ali wild with worry. He kissed each of them on both cheeks in relief.

Aksil was nowhere to be found.

Chapter Fourteen
The Slaves

During the daily quiet periods, when the afternoon sun was most brutal and the temperatures were unbearably high, the caravan shut down completely. Most of the traders, merchants and soldiers used that time to sleep in the shade of their tents. Although it was warm then, it was a relief from the brutal temperature reached in the sun each afternoon in the desert.

The slaves were forced to rest in the same tents with the camels, since the traders did not want either the slaves or the camels to lose too much fat or muscle out in the hot sun. A putrid smell arose from a combination of camel droppings, stomach gas, slave sweat and days on end without bathing. As Ali said, "It smells like a room full of animal carcasses that has been sealed for a year."

Ricardo prepared a paste made of blackberries, sage and the bark of the Adler tree to help heal the tender skin on Martim's ankle. All slaves were forced to wear an anklet with their master's name on it, and Martim's felt uncomfortable as it rubbed against his skin.

Ricardo and Martim used the rest period each day to learn more about each other, and they soon became quite close. Martim wound string around an avocado pit, and he and Ricardo would kick the object back and forth, keeping it in the air as long as possible. Once they counted more than 118 kick-touches before the *Qadamy*, as they called it, fell to the tent floor.

Ricardo taught Martim basic Spanish, and Martim taught Ricardo phrases in both Arabic and *Jula*, the language of the Mandinke. Ricardo regaled his friend with stories about Madrid, his family, the hospital and much more. They wrestled for fun.

One afternoon, Martim asked if he could invite two of his Mandinke friends to join them in their games.

Kebba and Abu were teenagers from Martim's village. They were bright, athletic and friendly – and they knew that they would be sold into slavery when they reached Cairo.

Often, the slaves were kept in warehouses or holding pens, but in the Sahara, they were allowed to be unshackled because the traders knew there was no potential for escape. Far from their home villages, the slaves' only chance of survival was to stay with the caravan.

While their traders were sleeping in the afternoon heat, the boys were not missed. Ricardo applied the paste to each of their ankles as he had for Martim, and it eased the boys' pain immediately. Martim and Ricardo taught the boys how to play Qadamy. With Martim as translator, Ricardo shared stories about the cities of Europe, of their schools, hospitals and parks. At first, the boys did not believe Ricardo when he spoke about being able to move at will between cities, and even countries, and about the many joys of being free.

Ricardo told Kebba, Abu and Martim that slavery was

wrong, and that in parts of the world it was against the law. He said that his parents taught him that all people were created in God's image, and that all, no matter what color, religion or nationality, were equal. He spoke of free will. The boys were stunned! They had been taught that they were born to be slaves, and they were doomed to live a life far beneath that of the traders, merchants, farmers, and even the soldiers. They had no free will!

The word of the tent sessions spread quietly but rapidly through the Mandinke slaves. Soon, there were more than twenty boys jammed in their tent each afternoon.

Ricardo had an idea. While he realized that escape would be difficult, it was possible. And even a slight chance to be free was better than being sold into a life of despair at the slave market in Cairo.

"Let us keep these meetings secret. We will train in the basics of martial arts that I learned from the jungle warriors. We will learn about survival in the desert.

Then each of you will bring other Mandinke to your own afternoon tents and, with our help, you will teach them.

Do not raise suspicion from the traders. Be agreeable and helpful at all times. In a month or so, we will have a small army of Mandinke slaves.

"Let each slave know where the weapons are kept. For now, we will train with sticks and broom handles. If any master knows of this plan, we could all be killed; success depends on trust and secrecy."

Every day, the twenty boys trained with great enthusiasm. Then they invited their friends to join their tent brigade. Soon, more than 200 Mandinke slaves were involved and, amazingly, no one else in the caravan was aware – or so Ricardo thought.

Martim and Ricardo decided that when they stopped at Ziz, the next oasis, the slave army would revolt.

At mid-afternoon, while the traders were sleeping, the boys entered their tents, tied them up and took their weapons. They fed and watered the camels, took food, supplies and goat skins filled with water for themselves, and loaded them on the camels. The boys freed more than 100 women and children slaves, who went with them as they headed back toward Timbuktu and, hopefully, their villages.

Their plan was to tell passing caravans and Arabs at the oases that there was someone with the plague in their group, so it would be best to stay away.

Ricardo was very happy that he could help in this slave rebellion. He often told Martim how he felt about slavery. "It is wrong, and I will not simply sit back and do nothing about it." He knew his parents would be proud of him for standing up to this injustice.

Martim led the revolt and the trip back west. He wanted to see his mother again, and after hearing from Ricardo how wonderful it was to be free, he would accept no other life.

Ricardo did not join the revolt. Instead, he had Martim tie him up in his tent, to be discovered later by Ali and the rest of the traders. Martim hugged him and gave him a small Mandinke amulet before he left. "May the spirit of Mansa Musa watch over you, Ricardo. We will be brothers forever."

Ricardo stayed with the caravan and its remaining 900 camels, and planned to continue on to Cairo and then Jerusalem.

Chapter Fifteen
On to Cairo

li and Ricardo spent the last weeks of the caravan trip together, especially at mealtime. Ricardo wanted to learn all he could about Ali's life and the culture of the Arab and the Dyula people. The Dyula's desert existence was very different than that of Ricardo and his family's back home in Spain. Everything depended on water and the collection, conservation and careful use of this most precious resource. Although oasis towns like Timbuktu were fertile and lush, some Dyula elders claimed that the desert was slowly creeping into their oasis paradise. These leaders worried that if there were not some planning for the future, Timbuktu would be swallowed up by the mighty Sahara. Most of the people felt these leaders were alarmists!

Ali believed in *animism* and thought animals, plants, rocks, thunder, shadows and more had a soul or spirit. He respected and honored all of nature. Ali held different beliefs than most of the people of the Sahara, who were Muslims, so in order for Ali and his family to survive and prosper in their community, they had to learn and respect the ways of Islam. They learned the five pillars of Islam: Declaration of Faith, Obligatory Prayer, Compulsory Giving, Fasting during the Month of Ramadan, and Pilgrimage to Mecca.

What Ali and Ricardo had in common was that they both loved their families very much.

On the final night of their journey, the caravan camped near the top of a limestone cliff on the west bank of the Nile River, near the Giza Pyramid. Guarding this Necropolis, or "city of the dead," was the Great Sphinx with the body of a lion and the head of a human. Ali regaled Ricardo with tales of the Great Pharaohs and of times of splendor and riches in Egypt. He told the story of how the Jewish people were slaves in Egypt until the pharaoh finally let them go on to

Israel. Ricardo thought he recognized a story like this from his early childhood.

Ali led Ricardo into a chamber of the Giza Pyramid where they saw mysterious hieroglyphs written in red paint. There were elaborately carved tombs in the chamber, where the pharaohs and their families were buried. Ali explained that the pharaohs were often buried with jewels and gold, with chariots and even unfortunately, with their slaves. Tomb raiders had pilfered most of the riches, but Ricardo could imagine the filled chambers in all their splendor.

As they walked back to their tents, Ali turned to Ricardo, "I know that you helped the slaves escape. I observed the boys in your tent learning martial arts and overheard your escape plans." So, Ali had known about the escape and never said a word – not to others in the caravan and certainly not to Ricardo.

"Why didn't you try to stop me, Ali?"

"Because I believed you when you explained that slavery is wrong, that we all should live as free men and women, and that all people were created in God's image. Ricardo, I am old now and while I can't change my people or their way of life, I can do my part to help right this wrong. However Ricardo, I need to warn you that others in the caravan know that you led this revolt and they plan to arrest you when we get to Cairo. They plan to sell you at the slave market!"

"What should I do, Ali?"

"There is no moon tonight. Take Kelen and go. I have packed food and water for you. I have arranged for you to meet my cousin Jatoo who will accompany you to Jerusalem. Go quickly now, Ricardo!"

"Thank you, Ali. I will never forget you or this kindness."

"Take this, Ricardo," Ali said, handing him a date palm seed. "Plant it in your home in Madrid and think of me."

As Ali turned and walked away, Ricardo put the seed in his pocket, then began to journey toward Cairo with Kelen.

Before sunrise, after traveling all night, Ricardo heard moaning and crying emanating from a wooden building with no windows. He knew it was one of the warehouses where they kept the slaves before the slave market. The door was closed, and a man was guarding it. He was sitting on the ground with his feet propped up on a rock, fast asleep. Ricardo silently slipped past the guard, unlocked the door, and peered in. Hundreds of eyes looked back at him. Ricardo put his finger to his lips and waved the enslaved men, women and children out of the building. They scattered throughout the city as Ricardo and Kelen moved on to meet Jatoo.

"This was not the way I envisioned visiting the third city on my map, but at least I made the most of it," Ricardo reflected.

JERUSALEM

Chapter Sixteen
On to Jerusalem

atoo was short and wide, with gray hair and a matching beard that flowed down to his expansive belly. While his stomach was the dominant aspect of his appearance, there was much more to him than that. He was an educated and intelligent man, a professor at the famous Al Azhar University in Cairo, who specialized in the history of the Middle East. A virtual encyclopedia of facts, dates and wonderful stories about the pharaohs, the rise and fall of civilizations, and the importance of Judaism, Christianity and Islam to the world, Jatoo knew about discoveries, inventions and philosophies that had changed the world. He taught his students about exciting new inventions like spectacles, windmills and the compass. He excitedly told them about gunpowder, which had recently been developed in China. And he spoke of scientists and thinkers like Aristotle and Archimedes. Ricardo knew immediately that traveling with Jatoo would be an unforgettable experience.

"As we travel toward Jerusalem," Jatoo said, "we will trace some of the story of the Jew's exodus from Egypt."

Jatoo told Ricardo that he had Jewish friends at the university who celebrated the holiday *Pesach* with a Passover *seder* each spring. "A seder was a ceremony to remember the Jews' escape from slavery in Egypt several thousand years ago," he explained.

"While it is difficult to know the exact details of what happened so long ago, we do know that the Jewish people were slaves in Egypt for hundreds of years under the thumb of the pharaohs and their armies. Moses, the leader of the Jewish people, along with his brother Aaron, went before Pharaoh Thutmose II. They said that God had spoken to Moses, commanding him to tell the pharaoh to "let our people go."

When Pharaoh refused, God brought plagues upon the Egyptians, ranging from blood flowing in the River Nile to painful boils, swarms of locusts, and more. With each plague, the pharaoh continued to refuse to free the Jews – until the tenth plague, when the pharaoh's son and each Egyptian firstborn son died. In his grief, Pharaoh finally relented and the Jews were set free to cross the Red Sea toward the land of Israel.

Stories of miracles along the way included a cloud that continually led them to water, *manna*, a bread, coming down from heaven to help feed them, and the parting of the Red Sea to help the Jews escape and destroy the pharaoh's army. Ricardo was quite young when his grandparents mysteriously disappeared from his life, but he did recall celebrating Passover in their home. He could still taste the dry *matzah*, unleavened bread, and his first sip of sweet red wine with his family around the table. He also remembered how each seder guest read about the Jew's historic journey, and how Nana held his face in both her hands, looked into his eyes, and exhorted, "Ricardo, never ever forget this story! It is part of our people's memory forever!"

Whereas Ricardo, Jatoo and Kelen traveled for ten days from Cairo to Jerusalem, it was suggested that the Jews wandered in the desert for forty years before they finally reached Israel.

Throughout those ten days, Ricardo never stopped questioning Professor Jatoo about the wondrous history of the area. He also began to question himself about his background and his religion. Because no religion was practiced in his home, he had never really thought about religion before. Every Easter and Christmas, the family went to the Catholic Church at the end of the street, always under the watchful eye of the community church organizer. "Non-believers" were punished and failure to attend church on those two holy days was considered an unforgivable sin. Ricardo often wondered why his parents only mouthed the words "savior" and "Jesus" during the services, never saying them out loud.

When Ricardo and Jatoo reached the walls of Jerusalem, there was fighting in front of the Zion Gate, so they moved on to the next gate, where archers were camped. Jatoo motioned for their little band to follow him farther, leading them to a patch of ground on the side of a hill that was covered in thorn bushes. He carefully parted some of the bushes and exposed the opening to a secret tunnel.

Jatoo explained, "This tunnel was cut out of rock during the reign of King Hezekiah nearly two thousand years ago to protect against an Assyrian invasion of Judah. Just follow it underground until you reach the end. You will then be near the wall of the Holy Temple near the center of Jerusalem."

Jatoo continued, "This is where we say goodbye, Ricardo. You are a fine young man, and I wish you well."

Jatoo took Ricardo by the arm and said, "Kelen will not be safe with you in the cities as you continue your journey. May I take him back home with me to care for and protect him until you return?"

The suddenness of this farewell shook Ricardo for a moment, but reflecting on the potential dangers that might lie ahead, he agreed to part with his beloved camel. Ricardo tearfully hugged Kelen and promised to return for him. "In this life or the next," he whispered in Kelen's ear. Kelen rubbed his face against Ricardo's and licked his cheek. It was a sad goodbye.

Jatoo handed Ricardo a slip of paper and said, "This is the first page of Genesis from the Hebrew bible. I thought you might want to learn more about your ancestors, Ricardo. Now go!"

Ricardo looked down at the paper and read, "In the beginning..."

He looked up, but Jatoo and the animals had already turned to head back to Cairo.

Chapter Seventeen
Mercy

icardo slogged through the tunnel, slowly making his way through ankle deep water until he emerged near the wall of the Holy Temple. He saw people praying, all facing the wall. Although the men and women were separated, they seemed to be praying with equal reverence and intensity. Many were crying – in fact, some were sobbing uncontrollably. Ricardo wondered if something had happened to cause such heartbreak.

The men were dressed in long robes and sandals. Most wore beards, and some had side locks of hair. Many wore turban-like head coverings. The women were also in long robes, some with veils and headscarves as a token of modesty.

Jerusalem was a small city within its walls, covering only one square kilometer in total size. It was roughly divided into four areas: Armenian, Muslim, Christian and Jewish. Ricardo was in the Jewish part surrounded by many synagogues and religious orders.

Standing before the Wall, the remaining wall of the destroyed Second Temple, in the heart of the historic and holy city of Jerusalem, Ricardo felt energized by its beauty and its spirituality. He thought, "Here I am, only fifteen years old and standing in the center of the world! I wonder what will be my next adventure?"

It only took a few moments for Ricardo to learn the answer to that question. There was a tap on his shoulder, and Ricardo turned to face a woman in ragged clothes with a baby in her arms, and her palm open to Ricardo.

She pleaded, "Please, we are starving! Can you give us some money for food?"

"I have no money," Ricardo replied, "but I will share my

food with you and your baby."

"Thank you, sir. Could we do it away from the sun and the heat? I have a shaded area in back of that building."

The woman led Ricardo through a narrow alley to a rickety structure made of wood and straw that was packed with mud. The woman went inside and handed the baby to Ricardo while she made room for them to sit in the very cramped quarters.

"Sir, what do you have to eat? I see that you are not really a sir, but just a boy. There is hardly a hair on your face!"

As Ricardo opened the food package that Jatoo had given him, he said, "I have some cheese, jam, bread and water." He offered the bread to the woman, and she grabbed it and bit into the end.

Ricardo asked, "What can your baby eat?"

She laughed, showing her dazzling white teeth and her red lips. She was, in fact, quite beautiful.

"My baby does not need food!"

Then she pulled back the blanket wrapped around her

baby to reveal a wooden block with a patch of hair and some painted eyes. "I fare better begging near the Temple when I hold my 'baby' in my arms," she explained. "You are a stranger here. Where are you from?"

"I come from Madrid, Spain, and my name is Ricardo. This is my first day in Jerusalem."

"You will be easy prey for my friends, Ricardo. They will eat you up and spit you out with only your eyeballs and your teeth remaining."

"What do you mean, miss? And what is your name?"

"My name is Mercy. My family and I belong to the *Dom* people. Some people call us *Gypsies*, but we don't like that name. It's an insult to us."

"I have heard the term gypsy, but never the word Dom before," said Ricardo.

"My people immigrated here from northern India more than one hundred years ago, because we were not welcome there. We became nomads, and even now we often move from place to place," Mercy explained. "While most of us work hard as blacksmiths, metal workers, and day laborers, some others are fortune tellers, sorcerers, and animal trainers who often perform at weddings and celebrations, and some come away from those events with fat pockets from the guests." She continued, "Those Dom are the ones who could take advantage of you, Ricardo. Whatever is in your pack would be gone in the blink of an eye."

Ricardo thought immediately of his father's medical pack and shuddered at the thought of losing something so precious.

"You said that you have no money," Mercy stated. "May I assume that you have no place to stay either, Ricardo?"

He nodded solemnly.

"Then you will fit right in with my friends and family," offered Mercy.

When they walked past the Wall on the way to her family's camp, Ricardo asked Mercy, "Why are so many people crying?"

"They are mourning the destruction of the Temple. It is a sad day for the Jews. It is called *Tisha B'Av.*"

Ricardo felt a stabbing pain in his chest when he heard a

rabbi call out, "O God, thy holy temple they have destroyed; they have laid Jerusalem in heaps."

Chapter Eighteen
The Dom Family

icardo and Mercy walked through a long winding Souk, or Arab market, on the way to the Dom camp, located near the Zion Gate. Jerusalem's story has been filled with many tales about conquerors destroying Jerusalem's fortifications, then rebuilding new ones. King David's son Solomon built the first temple on a hillside above the city on the Temple Mount, then extended the city's walls to protect the Temple. There had been no new walls for the last 200 years. Ricardo and Mercy walked by the only protected areas, the Temple Mount and the Citadel.

As they walked, Mercy told Ricardo more about her

people, "We fled persecution in India and moved west to Europe and the Middle East. My ancestors would stay in a country for as long as they felt safe, found food and some comfort. And when the comforts waned, they packed up their meager belongings and moved on.

"Because we are different, we were not accepted in many communities. As a result, our children were not allowed in the public schools, or if they were, they were often teased by the other children and even by the teachers. Most of our children dropped out of school after a while, and without an education, it was difficult to find respectable work. Many of us ended up on the streets," Mercy recounted sadly.

"I remember my father chiding my brothers and me, 'the street is the best school; learn about life from the street.'"

They were almost to the Dom camp when Mercy turned to Ricardo, "Let me give you fair warning, Ricardo. We have large families. I have five brothers and four sisters. We live together with our mother and father in one house. We all have a lot to say all of the time, and when we are together, our voices can get really loud. My friend once asked me, 'If everyone in your family is always talking, who is listening?'

"Tonight will be a real education for you, my young friend. We are entertaining at a religious ceremony in the early evening, then later tonight my sister Afrah will marry a boy from another Dom clan. Afrah is thirteen; her groom has just turned sixteen. They are expected to start having babies within the first year of their marriage. If they don't, the family will be disappointed."

After a nap and a bath, Ricardo felt refreshed and ready for the night's activities. Once Mercy entered the room, he went from being just ready, to being excited to go. With her hair washed and curled and her black sparkling eyes accented by a dark liner, she looked like a princess. Her lips were touched with a carmine color gloss. She wore a costume made of satin and lace, with little bells dangling from the sleeves and her ankles, which would jingle when she danced. For the second time in a day, Ricardo was truly moved by her.

First, they witnessed a christening of the son of a prominent Christian family. The church hall was decorated for the occasion with white flowers everywhere. The Dom clan provided the musicians, dancers and other types of entertainment. There was a trained brown bear and several clowns to please the children. Dispersed throughout the crowd were Dom magicians and fortunetellers. There were also several skilled thieves who roamed through the audience while their friends and family acrobats were performing their high-wire and tightrope acts.

Afrah's wedding was a beautiful, yet raucous, affair. While the men drank heavily, the women who were not permitted to drink alcohol, so they danced and sang throughout the night. Several of Mercy's brothers thought it would be fun to ply her young and inexperienced new friend with drink, so they introduced Ricardo to a series of drinking games. One game was particularly difficult for Ricardo. He and the brothers sat in a circle with a cup in the middle of them. The object of the game was to throw a coin into the cup. The person who accomplished that difficult task was able to choose one of the other drinkers to down their beer, and proving it by turning over his glass. Mercy's brothers had played this game many times before, and as each of them tossed their coin into the cup; they all seemed to choose Ricardo as their favorite beer drinker. Later, Ricardo would pay a heavy price for this foolishness.

When the party finally ended at sunrise, Ricardo leaned over a fence and vomited hunks of goat meat floating in alcohol. His stomach and throat burned like hot coals, and he swore he would never drink again. Mercy wiped Ricardo's forehead and mouth with a wet cloth, and led him to her family's tent, where she gently took off his vomit-laden robe and watched him fall into a deep sleep.

Chapter Nineteen
Mercy and Ricardo Roam the City

ercy and Ricardo spent most of the next two weeks together, except for the time each evening when Mercy went begging with her "baby." Her family welcomed Ricardo. They shared their food and their modest accommodations with him, and all they asked of Ricardo in return, were stories of his life and his family in Spain.

Ricardo noticed that many of the Dom children were constantly scratching ugly round sores on their scalps, arms and legs. When he questioned Mercy about it, she explained that their neighbors called the condition "Dom Disease," and that the community elders considered it a curse put on them by rival clans.

Ricardo scanned his father's medical notes for possible clues to this strange affliction. Under *skin conditions: children*, he found the following:

Tinea [Ringworm]. Scaly, crusty rash, appears as red round patches in scalp and body. Very contagious. Spreads rapidly among children. Remedy: Clean rash thoroughly 2x/day, then wash with Apple Cider Vinegar. Add an Aloe vera salve, which includes tea tree, turmeric and heated coconut oils. Important to wash hands often. Do not let children share combs, brushes, bedding or clothing. Wash same daily.

Ricardo told Mercy's father, Pali, who was a Dom elder, that he might be able to help get rid of this scourge. Pali called all the clan's children into the center of the camp, and he, Mercy and Ricardo checked their scalps and bodies for the telltale sores. Pali sent his scavengers out to find apple cider vinegar as Ricardo prepared a salve with ingredients from his pack.

The children's mothers were given strict orders to bathe

until the Romans destroyed it. Mercy asked Ricardo to imagine King David, King Solomon and the people from the Bible walking the same steps they were walking now. They saw people from all over the world praying and placing notes to God in the cracks between the stones of the Wall.

Ricardo especially enjoyed visiting the small walled-in Armenian section of the city, with the Tower of David and so many churches, merchants and artisans crammed together. He loved Jerusalem, and he especially loved the diversity of cultures and how the Muslims, Armenians, Christians and Jews all got along so well...except when they didn't!

Chapter Twenty
Mercy and Ricardo Face Reality

ach day, Ricardo learned a bit more about Mercy. They were sitting on steps overlooking the Mount of Olives when Mercy bore her soul to him. When she had just turned thirteen, her parents arranged for her to marry a distant cousin, Aishe. Mercy had known him since they were small children and had always despised him.

All of Mercy's cousins were afraid of Aishe. Whenever they were together, he took their coins, their food and the few toys they owned away from them. Because he was so much bigger than the rest of the children, even as a child, no one dared to stand up to him – except for Mercy – and he enjoyed making her pay for her bravery.

Mercy recounted that Aishe was now seventeen years old, very tall and quite muscular. And he behaved as he always had, hurting and bullying others. To make matters worse, the adults thought he was a nice young man since he was always polite and kind around them.

Mercy tried to argue with her father, Pali, to stop the engagement, but he told her that the agreement with Aishe's father was final and he would not change his decision. Mercy tried to look at the betrothal in a positive way, but on the night of their engagement party, Aishe got drunk and beat her. She fought back with all her strength, but he was just too powerful. Aishe warned her, "Soon I will be your husband, and you will do whatever I ask, whenever I ask it."

Aishe had mistreated her ever since, especially when Mercy did not bring home much money from an evening of begging. "You are so lazy," he would say. "Work harder or work more hours, I don't care, just bring in the money." Mercy said Aishe always hit her in her chest, stomach or back – places on her body that would not show the many bruises he caused.

Two days before Ricardo first met Mercy at the Wall, Aishe and his father left Jerusalem to attend a world meeting of Dom leaders in Rome. They planned to be away for more than a month.

Ricardo was devastated by Mercy's story. He truly admired her and knew that when they were together he felt comfortable, yet vitalized. He felt content. Mercy was the best friend he had ever had.

"Mercy, you do not have to marry Aishe. He is an evil person. You deserve so much better – certainly not to be beaten. I know that I would treat you only with tenderness and respect," Ricardo said as he took Mercy's hand in his.

"I am sure you would, Ricardo. But that is impossible."

"Let's be together. Come with me on my journey. Share life's wonders with me, Mercy."

"You are sweet, Ricardo. I could never do that to my family."

For the next two weeks, Ricardo and Mercy spent their days together, sharing everything.

At dinner one night, Pali whispered to Ricardo and Mercy that he needed to speak with them alone. Once outside, he put his arms around them and said, "Ricardo, you have been a blessing to our family these past weeks. Mercy is my happy, loving daughter again since you are with us. But it is time to let life's hard reality sink in. Aishe is on his way home. If he finds out how close you and Mercy have become, he will hurt you both, and the clan will not blame him."

"But Pali, he beats her. Have you seen her bruises? Mercy hates him. Please stop the marriage."

"Yes, I now know what a bad person Aishe is. He fooled us all! It pains me deeply to see my daughter so unhappy, but that is fate! Perhaps once they are married and have children, he will treat her better," Pali replied in an unconvincing voice.

Ricardo looked into Mercy's eyes and said, "Please, come away with me."

Mercy avoided his gaze and hung her head, saying, "Ricardo, I am promised to another, whether I like it or not.

My father is right. Aishe will track us down. This has been a beautiful dream for me. The dream is now over. You must go."

Pali left them alone for their goodbyes. Ricardo tried to give Mercy his diamond, but she refused, saying, "This was given to you to build your future upon, not mine. Instead, let's leave each other a permanent sign of remembrance for each other."

Taking out a small sharp blade, Mercy told Ricardo to turn his head, and proceeded to cut a tiny "M" behind his left ear. She then lifted her hair and had Ricardo cut an "R" behind her right ear.

"We are forever marked and forever bonded, Ricardo. You will always be in my heart," Mercy cried tearfully.

Pali came back with Ricardo's pack and medical pouch. He also handed Ricardo a small bag of bread, dates and some coins for his journey. He put his arms around them both once again, this time gently bringing their foreheads together. All three of them were crying at their parting.

Ricardo ran to the Wall, and placed a note to God in between its ancient stones. The tear-stained note asked for Mercy's safety and for the opportunity for them to someday meet again.

INDIA

Chapter Twenty-One

Asta

he trip to India took several weeks by boat along a route of ancient maritime traders down the Red Sea through a narrow passage into and across the Indian Ocean. The voyage was a total blur to Ricardo, as he was bereft from his abrupt separation from Mercy. He was also beginning to get homesick for his family.

Ricardo snapped out of his sadness as the boat entered the Bay of Bengal along the northeastern tip of the ocean and a huge tropical cyclone seemed to swallow them up completely. The sea changed from choppy to rough to waves forty meters high. The cyclone turned them around in a clockwise direction, virtually lifting their boat completely out of the water. The wind carried the rain along like the tails of a whip, stinging their faces as it beat against them. Ricardo thought about Carlo, the cook on the Aviela, and how his father saved him by tying him to a cask. While others on the ship panicked, Ricardo calmly tied himself to the ship's mast and tried to breathe slowly, meditating about his family and his wonderful experiences on his journey thus far. There was screaming and praying among the passengers and crew, and then – just as abruptly as it came – the storm passed. The bay was smooth once again, and while the ship had suffered some leaks and lost some freight overboard, all else seemed to be intact.

The captain turned the ship back toward the port near Saptagram, the capital of Southern Bengal. As Ricardo untied himself, he once again felt energized and lucky to be alive.

Saptagram was a very crowded and active city and just a short walk to the Ganges River. Wonderful bright colors abounded amid unfamiliar sounds and smells and throngs of people. As soon as Ricardo arrived at the Ganges, he witnessed a colorful Hindu funeral. First, he saw the procession of family and friends of the deceased to the cremation ground. The body was laid on a pile of wood on a raft, which was then lit on fire by the deceased's eldest son. As Ricardo watched the burning funeral pyre float down river, he heard his name being called out of the crowd.

"Ricardo! Ricardo Columbo!"

And exactly as Señor Vasquez described, Ricardo was called to the side of the sadhu Asta. Ricardo felt drawn, almost hypnotized, by this little man with his bare chest and white loincloth sitting on a wooden raft in the Ganges River.

"Ricardo, you can make a difference in this world," Asta said. "You are one of the few who can change things. You bear a great responsibility. Listen and learn."

As he had done with Señor Vasquez, Asta spent the following days teaching Ricardo about India and its history, traditions and beauty. He also shared stories of the many religions and sects in India, particularly about his religion, Hinduism. Ricardo learned about the ways of the sadhus. Sadly, he also witnessed the divisive caste system and the terrible life of the *untouchables*, regarded as the lowest people in all of India.

"I know that many months ago in Madrid," Asta recounted, "my old friend Mateo gave you the map that led you to me. He shared that I was a sadhu, a Hindu holy man. I am the reincarnation of Valmiki, a great sage and famous author from ages ago. Let me explain about sadhus. Sadhus are expected to adopt a totally ascetic life, practicing strict self-denial and even begging for our food. We must leave our homes and families, shave most of the hair on our bodies, and live naked or in loincloths. We survive primarily on the charity of others, perform acts of worship and self-purification, and serve those who are needy. There are millions of us in India today, Ricardo."

He continued, "Most of us that you see on the streets begging, telling fortunes, performing exorcisms, casting spells, juggling or selling herbs and potions are sadhus. Also we are well known for making amulets to protect against the forces of evil."

After nearly a week of meditation and instruction from

Asta, Ricardo was assigned two young sadhu novices to guide him through the many customs and rituals he would encounter, and to help him with the *Bengali* and *Hindi* languages. Ricardo liked them both immediately. Arjun and Aditya were twin boys who were orphaned at birth and raised in Asta's monastery. They were now 15 years old, and very bonded to one another. They completed each other's sentences, and when one was sick or hurt, the other felt his brother's pain or discomfort.

"Your work here in India will be not unlike what you did in the Sahara for the Mandinke slaves," Asta said. "You will live with, educate and inspire the outcasts here in Saptagram. You will teach them about freedom, equality and self-worth. You will set an example for them about better hygiene and healthier living."

Ricardo protested, "There are thousands upon thousands of untouchables here, Asta. Most do not know how to read, write or even count. They have been kept so low for so long. What chance do I have to do what you ask?"

Asta answered, "You are a great novelty here, Ricardo.

Because you are an educated European with medical skills, many will be in awe of you and thus listen to you. But be wary of the Brahmin, our priests. They want to keep the untouchables down. By the way, the untouchables are not even considered a caste, they are outside of and below the caste system."

"I do not understand why there is such a horrible thing as the caste system. Why does it even exist?" asked Ricardo.

"I believe it is a way to keep the poor and uneducated, poor and uneducated," Asta replied.

"Many Hindus and Buddhists believe that untouchables were unclean in the eyes of their gods. The life of an untouchable is unbearable. They are forced to do work that no one else would do, like killing rats, skinning and rendering animal carcasses, removing cow dung from the streets, and cleaning latrines. Untouchables also prepare bodies for funerals. They are forbidden to eat their meals with, pray with or marry someone from a higher caste. They live in dirt hovels, experience constant insults and indignities – and Ricardo, you can help change some of that.

"Now, go with Arjun and Aditya, and remember, you are the chosen son of Mateo Vasquez. Follow your map, help change things along the way, and always remember, Ricardo, it is all *B'Sheret*.

When Ricardo looked at him in surprise, Asta continued, "And don't look so shocked that a sadhu can speak Hebrew. Here in India, in Cochin and Saptagram, are Jews from one of the lost tribes of Israel."

Chapter Twenty-Two
The Slums

As the twins led Ricardo from the Ganges, they passed magnificent palaces with tall gates that protected spiral towers and sprawling gardens. Hundreds of workers scurried about the grounds as servants, gardeners or guards. Ricardo had never seen such opulence and wealth before.

Continuing farther beyond the mansions, however, Ricardo was greeted by the smell of rotten sewage that burned his eyes and the back of his throat. He fought an urge to vomit by breathing calmly and slowly as Asta had taught him. The stench was emanating from an area of dilapidated shacks in a low-lying valley stretching as far as Ricardo could see. In the center of this valley was a large garbage dump, which was filled not only with garbage, but also with human waste from the upper castes. Narrow, muddy paths ran from the entrance of this slum to the dump. It was a place unfit for human habitation, yet it was the home to the untouchables.

Asta's prediction that Ricardo would generate a reaction from the residents of the slum was an understatement. While some hid in their bamboo huts, most came out to see and even touch this foreigner. Arjun and Aditya introduced him to Giona Bellami, a worn and wrinkled doctor who had been working to heal the children of the slum for more than twenty years. He had come to India from Italy on a holiday trip and never left. Appalled by the conditions of the untouchable children, he simply felt that he had to do something – to improve their dire situation.

"Ricardo, the conditions in the slum are beyond belief," explained the doctor. "There is no sewage or waste disposal. People defecate outside of their huts and wait for it to be washed away twice a year in the monsoons. Because the slum is in a valley, when the heavy rains come, the waste often flows inside their huts and contaminates their meager belongings.

"In addition, the water supply is tainted, mainly because these untouchables are not allowed to draw water from the main spring-fed wells in the center of town. Their water comes from a disgusting pond near the dump.

"Let me continue, Ricardo. There is no hospital or medical center here. If a child gets very sick, we try to keep them cool and wait to see if the child will live or die. I use herbs to help whoever I can, but I am just one person among thousands of these poor souls.

"The untouchable children are not allowed to go to school, so most do not read or write. Do you know that untouchables are not allowed to wear shoes? As a result, almost every child here has debilitating hookworms."

Giona told Ricardo that he had often thought of returning to his comfortable home in Milan, but could not bear the thought of leaving the children.

"This man deserves sainthood," thought Ricardo.

"I am here to help you, Dr. Bellami. Where do you want me to start?" asked Ricardo. He described his training both in the hospital and as a pharmacy apprentice, which he thought might be useful. He also thought he could help find medicinal healing plants and teach the parents about hygiene.

Giona explained to Ricardo that they needed to find a way to remove the waste from the huts, to have clean water, and to have proper drainage during the rainy seasons. He also wanted to relocate families away from the garbage dump, since it was a breeding ground for disease carried by flies, mosquitoes, cockroaches and rats.

"Because the untouchables are forced to take jobs, such as excrement removal, often moving human waste from the latrines in town with their bare hands, their situation is beyond desperate. It is obscene!"

Giona offered to share his hut and his food with Ricardo while the boy stayed in the slum. The first night together, they stayed up very late discussing how they could make a difference in the lives of the untouchables.

That night, Ricardo also learned there was another reason Giona wanted to stay in India. He had fallen in love with a nurse/midwife who helped deliver babies of the women in the slums. Her name was Anika.

Ricardo looked in his father's medical journal under worms and found this:

Hookworms: usually enter the body through the feet, caused by animal and human feces in soil. Symptoms: itching and rash common, coughing, abdominal pain, diarrhea and often fatigue. Treat with turmeric to reduce cramps and bloating, and kill worms. Also drink tonic made from black walnut and wormwood oils. Chew pumpkin seeds, carrots and cloves to expel worms.

Giona remarked that turmeric grew wild in India and was readily available. Arjun and Aditya travelled the neighboring woods with Ricardo and gathered a large quantity of turmeric. As they walked through the trees and grassy areas nearby, Ricardo showed them valuable medicinal plants that were at their fingertips.

"This is Aloe vera for burns. Next to that is *lemon grass* for sore throat and pain. On that hill is *mint*, used for cough, cold and diarrhea. Did you know that what you call *tulsi*, we call *basil*. In India, tulsi is called the *elixir of life*. It is used to treat headaches, stomach disorders, heart disease and even malaria. Tulsi can be planted as a repellent to flies, mosquitoes and other insects. It seems that India is a virtual haven for plants that will help cure whatever ails you," Ricardo said excitedly.

"Tomorrow, I want you to take me to where we can find lots of seaweed. If we replant it into our drinking pond, we may be able to clean up the water supply."

Chapter Twenty-Three

The Sultan of Delhi

aking the slum habitable proved a huge task that included improving the drainage and water supply, moving the garbage dump, and much more. Giona and Ricardo realized they would need tools, hundreds of workers, and the support of those in power – in this case, the Sultan of Delhi.

Giona asked Ricardo, "How in the world can we get a wealthy and powerful ruler like the sultan to listen to us?"

"We will do it by showing him how he and his sultanate will also benefit from these improvements."

Ricardo learned that for the past ten years there had been

a struggle for control of this region of India between this Muslim Sultan and his archenemy, the Hindu Maharaja. The sultan had encountered difficulty gaining the loyalty of the people because he was Muslim and most of his citizens were Hindu.

"I have a plan," Ricardo said. "Please give me a pen, some ink and your nicest paper."

In his very best handwriting, Ricardo wrote:

Dear Sultan and Great Ruler,

We have come to India from Italy and Spain and would consider it an honor if you would meet with us. We have an idea that might make your dynasty even more powerful.

Your humble servants, Doctor Giona Bellami and Ricardo Columbo

The twins delivered the note to the captain of the Guards situated at the palace gate.

The next morning, four palace guards in full armor marched through the mud of the slum to Giona's door. Ricardo and Giona were escorted to the palace, where they were told to undress and to get into a tub of very hot water.

Seconds later, four servants came with soap and brushes and proceeded to scrub their bodies head to toe. At first, Ricardo felt uncomfortable being washed by total strangers, but soon he was relaxed and cleaner than he had been since leaving his mother's home.

Beautiful silk clothes and slippers were laid out for them, and after dressing they were brought before the Sultan.

The sultan was a powerfully built man of around thirty with a large, black handlebar mustache. Draped around his neck and shoulders were dozens of necklaces of pearl, sapphire, jade and other precious jewels. Ricardo thought the Sultan must be quite strong to be able to even stand with all those jewels weighing him down. "Welcome to my palace, gentlemen," the Sultan said in a loud clear voice. "I am Muhammad Bin Tughlaq, the Sultan of Dehli. So much for the introductions, How can you help me strengthen my kingdom?"

Giona spoke first, telling the Sultan about the dreadful conditions in the slum, the dying children, and the utter despair experienced by those who lived there.

The Sultan seemed unmoved. "As far as I understand, the untouchables have lived that way for many years. Why would that be important to me now?"

Ricardo stepped forward.

"Because, Your Excellency, you may be overlooking a valuable ally. The Maharaja desperately wants to replace you in the seat of power. The Hindu leaders have treated the untouchables less than poorly over the years. The slum residents live in the worst possible conditions, and are prohibited from praying to their Hindu gods along with fellow Hindus of the higher castes. In part, because of this, the untouchables are sad and angry. They are waiting for a great king, or a god, to lead them from their desperate lives."

"And you European wise men think that king, that god, could be me."

"May I suggest one small act that would impact many, Great Sultan?"

"Go on, young man."

"Sandals. Give them all sandals to wear every day."

"Why? What will sandals do for them?"

"The untouchables are not allowed to wear shoes of any kind, as a symbol of their caste. As a result, most get worms from the soil, which enter through the soles of their feet and infest their bodies. This especially affects the children, and some even die from this preventable affliction. Sandals offer a simple solution to this terrible problem. The Hindu priests will be furious with you, but the people will love you."

"Interesting! Tell me more."

Giona spoke next.

"We believe that if you made a few easy changes in their lives, the people would become loyal subjects of your Sultanate. Some would even become Muslims and leave the low status assigned to them in Hinduism. They might do it for you initially, but over the years, they would likely follow the Five Pillars of Islam with devotion."

Now the Sultan was truly interested.

"The untouchables," Giona continued, "live in a low area, which floods during the monsoons. Because there is a garbage dump next to this area, their residences become a haven for disease. Ten minutes to the south there is a barren, hilly area. Relocate them! Dig some canals to move the waste, create a clean water supply, and make other basic improvements. I'm certain that if you led this noble effort, you would think of other wonderful things you could do as well."

"Do they also need a school?" the sultan asked.

"Yes!" Ricardo and Giona excitedly shouted excitedly in unison.

Ricardo realized the sultan recognized this opportunity to enhance his legacy without having to go to war. Instead, he would destroy his enemy through acts of kindness to his newfound subjects.

"It is brilliant. Let's do it! I will be personally in charge of the entire project. We will call the new development *Sultan of Delhi Park*.

"They will sing your praises here and throughout the world for ages," cried Ricardo.

The next morning, the sultan brought his chief builders and planners to the hills. Within a month, there were hundreds of dry bamboo and clay huts, each with a small kitchen and a separate latrine in back. There were deep drainage canals and proper roads. Most of the work was completed by previously unemployed untouchables as part of their new on-the-job training program. The untouchables were no longer limited to being rag pickers and human waste haulers. They were now carpenters, roofers, blacksmiths and road builders – and they were proud of it!

The crowning glories of Sultan of Delhi Park were a school, a medical center, and in the middle of it all, a large graceful mosque.

In a matter of months, there were few untouchables left in the recently plowed over slums. While most of the untouchables stayed true to their Hindu beliefs, there were many more Muslims praying to Allah in the hills.

And the upper castes were left to figure out how to get rid of their human waste!

Chapter Twenty-Four
Giona and Anika

iona remembered the first time he saw Anika. It was the middle of the monsoon season, and mud and rushing water were rising almost to his knees while he was performing a particularly difficult breech birth on a thirteen-year-old Hindu girl. Seemingly out of nowhere an angel, Anika, appeared beside him and skillfully turned the baby, allowing her to come into the world with a final push from her mother. The baby's loud cries were beautiful background music to Giona and Anika as their eyes met. In an instant, while they were savoring the joy of the birth and appreciating one another's skills, love bloomed.

Giona remembered from his earlier years in Italy, that they called this deep reaction upon a first meeting a *lightning strike*, as if each of the pair were hit by a bolt of lightning sent by the gods of love. Giona and Anika knew instantly they would somehow be together for the rest of their lives.

Anika was the daughter of an esteemed teacher of the *Bhagavad Gita*, part of Hindu scriptures. Written in Sanskrit many hundreds of years before, it was referred to as the *Gita*. It became the spiritual guiding light to scholars and religious leaders throughout India and Asia.

Anika's mother was one of the few woman administrators in their local government. While Anika's parents were pleased that she was trained as a nurse and midwife, they were not happy that she chose to practice her profession in the slums among the untouchables.

For the past six years, Giona and Anika had worked together trying to help those in their community who needed it the most. Out of respect to Anika's family during this time, they were never together outside of work. Anika said that her father would not allow them to be married, since her family was Hindu and Giona was a foreigner and decidedly not a Hindu.

Recently, Anika's family had begun pressuring her to marry and have children, so she told them about Giona. At first, her father forbade her from returning to work and from seeing Giona again, but over time, after learning what a respected doctor and person Giona was, he agreed to meet with him.

There, Anika's father warned Giona that if Anika married a non-believer, she would be banned from their family, would not be allowed to visit the Hindu temples or pilgrimage sites, and would be prevented from entering heaven. Giona knew how much Anika valued family and her religion, so he agreed to study the Hindu scriptures and convert to Hinduism if her father would give them his blessing. He also agreed to raise their children as Hindus. Anika's father had one last question for Giona. "Do you play chess, Giona? Chess originated in India more than 700 years ago, you know." Giona said, "Yes, I do indeed play chess."

Anika and Giona's wedding was a huge and colorful affair that lasted for three days. It began with a party given by Anika's family to welcome the groom and his family. Since Giona had no family in India, he asked Ricardo to stand in for them. Anika's hands and feet were painted with henna in intricate designs, and the guests began to dance and sing in the bride's honor.

A wedding altar covered with flowers was built especially for the ceremony, and in it's middle was a holy fire burning to bear witness to the wedding. The guests included people from different castes and religions, including both the Sultan of Delhi and the Maharaja. Each seemed to be trying to outdo the other with the splendor of their accompanying royal courts, and with the extravagant gifts they offered the bride and groom. The two men nodded to each other upon entering, and amazingly, were polite and respectful to each other. The Sultan departed soon after the ceremony ended, because he did not wish to be in a room when liquor was served.

To Ricardo's complete surprise, Giona rode up to the altar on a white horse. He looked quite regal! Anika was beautiful and elegant in her red and gold wedding sari. Giona and Anika exchanged floral garlands expressing their desire to be married to one another, then in a symbol of bonding, Anika's father poured water over their joined hands. Their garments were then tied together and they walked seven times around the ceremonial fire – each time around signifying a blessing and a request from the gods. Together, they said, "We have taken the seven steps. You have become mine forever!" It seemed quite similar to Ricardo's aunt's wedding that he had attended several years before in Madrid.

A red-orange powder was applied to Anika's hair which symbolized she was now a newly married woman. There was a prayer to *Ganesha*, the Hindu god of new beginnings and good fortune. Cords were tied to Giona and Anika's wrists to ward off difficulties they might encounter in their marriage, and Giona placed a black and gold necklace around Anika's neck so she would receive the blessings of happiness and prosperity. The guests, and there were many hundreds of them, threw rice on the happy couple.

Ricardo had never seen so much food. He learned that it

was traditional to combine sweet, salty, spicy, hot and pungent flavors at an Indian feast.

There was *palak chaat* (a crispy spinach) and *tandoori lamb*. Ricardo had grown accustomed to the hot seasonings of India, so he especially liked the spicy fish curry with chili and cumin. There were piles of *naan, kulcha, roti* and other breads, and several tables were filled with fresh fruits and desserts. As he had experienced over his months in India, Ricardo only reached for the food with his right hand, since the left was often used for bathroom purposes.

Several of Anika's friends urged Ricardo join them on the dance floor. He was soon singing Indian songs – even though he did not understand the words – and laughing until his sides hurt. The evening was an explosion of joy! Ricardo was elated for Giona and his beautiful bride, and was certain their marriage would follow the Hindu tradition to be "for life and forever." The world was a beautiful place that night.

Chapter Twenty-Five

Leaving India

The sultan appointed Giona and Anika chief medical advisers to his Sultanate. The positions came with a monthly salary and a home near the entrance to the Sultan of Delhi Park. The newlyweds worked at the new Sultan of Delhi Medical Center and were able to make enormous strides improving the health of the untouchables, especially the children. Hookworms were no longer a major issue, since now, the children all wore sandals. With Giona's weekly health education classes, the number of people who were sick or dying was greatly reduced. Ricardo and Anika helped teach the classes, which emphasized hand washing before every meal, bathing every other day, brushing teeth daily, and proper bathroom habits. The new wells, latrines and drainage system, along with distancing the community from the garbage dump, also helped reduce disease.

There were other wonderful changes as well. At dinner one night, Giona and Anika informed Ricardo that they were expecting a baby and they intended to name the child after him. Anika said, "If it is a boy, we are naming him Ricardo, and if it is a girl, her name will be Riki." Ricardo was thrilled for his friends and honored to be the baby's namesake.

"I wish I could be here for the birth and the baby naming," Ricardo said, "but it is time for me to continue my adventure. I want to be home by my seventeenth birthday, which is only a year away. You have been great friends, and I know we will meet again soon."

Ricardo commissioned a local tailor shop to make baby blankets – one pink with the name `Riki` embroidered on it in blue, and one light blue with the name `Ricardo` embroidered on it in white. Giona and Anika loved their very first baby gifts.

As a parting gift, the sultan gave Ricardo a jade necklace. He thanked Ricardo for opening his eyes to the responsibility he had to his subjects. "Quite frankly, Ricardo, I would rather be loved and appreciated than feared. I understand that next you will be traveling to China. Allow me to provide you with a military escort to assure you arrive safely in that secret and mysterious country." Ricardo thanked him for his kindness and left him by saying, "Great Sultan, I promise to tell others, in every country I visit, what you did for the untouchables here in India. Your name and good deeds will be an example for kings and princes all over the world." Before he departed, Ricardo put the necklace in the secret pocket of his jacket.

Ricardo's last farewell visit was to see Asta at the river. Asta hugged Ricardo and told him how proud he was of what he had accomplished in just a few short months. "God's mission for us on earth is to help make the world a safe and loving place for all who live here. My friend, the

Rabbi of Cochin, has a term for it: *Tikun Olum.* It means 'to heal the world.' You, my dear friend Ricardo, are destined to be a great healer." With those words, Asta was gone.

CHINA

The Trip to China
Chapter Twenty-Six

he sultan assigned the soldiers Ankur and Fareed to accompany Ricardo to China. They made arrangements to sail from the Bay of Bengal through the Strait of Malacca to the next city on Ricardo's map, Hangzhou, in the China Sea. Ricardo had his own cabin onboard the ship. He thought, "this is quite a difference from swabbing the decks of the Aviela." Ricardo was rarely left alone. Either Ankur or Fareed was always with him on alert to keep Ricardo out of danger. At the port of Kedah, Ricardo was watching the crew unload huge sacks of almonds when the rope holding the sacks suddenly snapped. The cargo was headed directly towards him, but Ankur dashed across the deck and threw himself at Ricardo, knocking him aside. The almonds fell on Ankur, crushing his right leg.

Ricardo was at Ankur's side immediately. He ripped Ankur's pant leg and saw that the leg was broken below the knee. Ankur was in intense pain, so Ricardo took out the bottle of *Alberto's Secret Formula* from his pack.

"Open your mouth, Ankur, here is something to ease your pain," he directed. "I am going to put your leg back in place and you may feel this." He pulled down on Ankur's leg and realigned the broken bones. Ricardo told Fareed to find some cloth and wood as he held the bones in place, and when Fareed returned, Ricardo carefully crafted a splint and wrapped it tightly with the cloth.

For the remaining three weeks onboard the ship, Ricardo made certain Ankur kept his leg elevated and wrapped.

Once the ship landed in Hangzhou – another city marked on his map – Ricardo accompanied Ankur to the hospital to check on what further needed to be done for his leg. The doctor told Ankur that his leg was set perfectly and that he should thank the ship's doctor for doing such a good job. Ankur responded, "Here is my ship's doctor. Ricardo reset my leg."

"I am quite impressed," the doctor said. "I have always been fascinated with western medicine, Ricardo. I am Doctor Mi-Yuan. Would you join my family and me for dinner tonight? Perhaps we could learn from each other."

"I would be honored to have dinner with you and your family, Doctor," Ricardo answered. "Perhaps you would be interested in my father's medical journal. He is a pharmacist, so most of the entries are about medicinal plants."

Ricardo's dinner with Mi-Yuan and his family was delightful. "There is a saying in China," Mi-Yuan said, "about our taste preferences in each part of our great country. The East is sweet, the South is salty, the West is sour and the North is hot." Mi-Yuan's wife, Genji, served a simple yet delicious meal of crispy duck with rice noodles. They drank *jiuniang*, a fermented soup made with sweet rice wine. Ricardo drew pictures of birds and fish with their three-year-old daughter, Bao."

After dinner, Mi-Yuan encouraged Ricardo to tell them about his family and life in Spain. After several minutes, Mi-Yuan asked if he could see the journal Ricardo mentioned earlier. With great pride and care, Ricardo pulled the book from his pack.

Mi-Yuan asked, "Ricardo, as one example, what does your journal say is a cure for diarrhea?" Ricardo read his father's notes: *The recommended remedies are mint and carrot juice with a touch of ginger, plus blackberries, chamomile tea, apple cider vinegar with peppermint. All of these help.*

"How do you treat it here in China?" Ricardo asked.

"Traditionally, we give hot peppermint tea or vegetable broth to avoid dehydration. Plain white rice is used to calm the stomach and firm the stools. We use herbal therapy and often add acupuncture treatments."

The conversation expanded to include many medical conditions and remedies. It continued late into the night and for several nights that followed.

Chapter Twenty-Seven
Dr. Mi-Yuan

icardo stayed with Mi-Yuan and his family for almost two weeks. Every day, he assisted the doctor at the hospital. He encountered difficulties with the Chinese medical system that were similar to those in Madrid. One day, as he and the doctor were leaving the hospital, Mi-Yuan confided in Ricardo, "I suspect that you noticed there are not enough qualified doctors or nurses on staff. Only the wealthiest patients can afford good medical care. Of course, sanitation is a problem, especially among the poor and less educated. Because of this, the hospitals and doctors have little chance against a major epidemic, like the plague.

He continued, "Ricardo, You seem to be comfortable both in the hospital setting and working with my patients. How would you like to continue here as my assistant for a year or two?" asked Mi-Yuan. "It would be great experience for you, and a blessing for me."

"Thank you so much, Mi-Yuan. While I am tempted to accept your kind offer, I have been away from my family for a long time and I miss them. I wish to return home. But I will carry with me all you have taught me about medicine and about China. I will never forget our visits to West Lake and to the Buddhist Cave carvings with your family. When I think of Hangzhou, I will recall the beautiful pagodas, temples and bridges, but mostly I will remember you."

While they were saying goodbye at the dock of the Grand Canal, Mi-Yuan handed Ricardo a letter of introduction addressed to Dr. Jai-Guo, the personal physician to the emperor of China.

Chapter Twenty-Eight
The Grand Canal

icardo booked passage on a paddleboat traveling from China's southernmost point in Hangzhou north to Dadu on the Grand Canal. Because there were several markings on his map around Dadu, Ricardo thought it must be an important city.

The trip on the oldest and longest manmade waterway took more than a week, and Ricardo fully enjoyed it on the Grand Canal. Work on this engineering marvel had begun nearly eighteen hundred years earlier in an effort to get grain and supplies to troops in the north fighting against invading Mongols. Not only was the canal a convenient way to transport supplies, but it also created a passage from north to south that was free from the storms and bandits plaguing the China Sea. The canal intersected the Yellow and the Yangtze Rivers, in effect connecting all of China. During the trip, the paddleboat captain explained to Ricardo that, over the years, more than one million people had been forced to work on building the canal.

The trip afforded Ricardo time to reflect on his journey so far. As he passed rice fields and farms along the river, he reminisced about Carlo and the captain of the Aviela, about Armoldo, Martim, Kelen and Ali and Jatoo. He fondly remembered his time in India with Asta, Giona and Anika. Above all, Ricardo thought about Mercy and what might have become of her.

"What an exciting and wonderful time this has been. But after China, I will be ready to return to Spain. It's time," he told himself.

Chapter Twenty-Nine
Ricardo Meets the Emperor

octor Jai-Guo greeted Ricardo warmly. "I am very fond of Doctor Mi-Yuan, both on a professional and personal basis. He is a wonderful physician and a very dear friend, and if you are his friend, you are mine as well," he said. "You are welcome here in Dadu, Ricardo."

"Thank you," replied Ricardo. "I am anxious to learn all I can about China."

Jai-Guo explained, "Our emperor loves to meet foreigners. He is best suited to tell you about our country."

The next afternoon, Jai-Guo presented Ricardo to the

emperor. "Great Emperor, may I introduce Ricardo Columbo from Madrid, Spain? Ricardo, this is Ukhaghatu Khan Toghon Temur, Emperor Huizong of the Yuan Dynasty, ruler of all China."

The emperor invited Ricardo and Doctor Mi-Yuan to an ornate lunch of *Rich and Noble Chicken,* a delicious dish of baked stuffed chicken wrapped in clay and lotus leaves. The emperor informed them, "China is an ancient country with many tales of folklore and legends. One such legend is about the bird we are eating at this moment. It seems that a starving beggar found a chicken, but didn't have a stove to cook it in. He was very hungry, but also quite innovative. He killed the chicken and covered it with mud, then baked it over a fire. An emperor of the Qin Dynasty was passing by, smelled the aroma of the baking chicken, stopped, and joined the beggar for dinner. The emperor enjoyed the dish so much that he instructed his cooks to add the recipe to the royal menu at the Imperial Court. Since that day, Rich and Noble Chicken has also been called *Beggar's Chicken.*"

As they finished their lunch, Emperor Toghon advised

Ricardo that the best way for him to understand China was to be out among its people.

"As you visit our greatest historical sites, like the *Great Wall* and the *Terra Cotta Army*, feel free to speak with our merchants, our farmers, our teachers and any people you meet along the way. Listen what they have to say, Ricardo, and report back to me. I am interested in hearing what you have seen and heard."

Ricardo took the emperor's advice. He spoke with dozens of people whom he met in the markets, hospitals and schools he visited. Most of them were complimentary of their leader. Some told Ricardo, in confidence, "Even though the emperor is not originally from China, he is a just and fair ruler." But the people did complain about how some of the government officials, specifically the tax collectors, stole from them and from the emperor. They exacted bribes, favored their own families and their religious leaders, and became rich and powerful at the expense of the people.

After four weeks traveling in the cities and the countryside, Ricardo returned to the palace to brief the emperor.

"Many of your representatives bully the citizens, take bribes, and demand unfair payment from merchants. Even the poorest farmers are threatened and forced to give up a portion of their meager crops to the officials. They are told that if they do complain, they will be punished. Some tax men give the tax money collected in your name to their own families and to leaders of their mosque, temple or church. I am sorry to bring you this disturbing news, Your Excellency, but if you do not address this situation, you may have a revolt among your people."

"What would you do if you were me, Ricardo?" the emperor asked.

"I have an idea on how to make things better. First of all, send people you trust to get evidence on the worst offenders among your representatives. Give them a public trial. If they have been stealing from you and your people, send them to prison. Then employ honest officials who do not have ties to the community they will administer. What if you chose Muslim and Christian officials to oversee areas of Han Chinese, and chose Chinese officials to supervise areas that were prominently Muslim? Didn't your grandfather, the great Kublai Khan, employ Marco Polo, a non-Chinese, as an administrator when he was in power? You could use the same strategy in areas that are Buddhist, Taoist or followers of Confucius. Bring in officials who do not have family or religious ties to the community. The bullying and bribery will almost certainly stop."

"It makes sense, Ricardo. Any other ideas?" asked the emperor.

"Yes, Your Excellency. Obviously, you care about your people. Let them know it. Go out into the streets and tell them your plan to make things better for them. Visit the universities and speak with the students. Tell them the days of bribery and intimidation are over. Ask for their help. They need to hear directly from you. The people will support you."

"How old are you, Ricardo?" asked the emperor.

"Sixteen, sir."

"You are wise beyond your age, my boy."

"Thank you, Your Excellency. Earlier this year, I helped

the sultan of Dehli with similar concerns about meeting the needs of his people." Ricardo offered.

Chapter Thirty
The Terracotta Army

s part of his education in China, the emperor recommended Ricardo visit the Terra Cotta Army in Shaanxi. He instructed Bin Li Wei, a scholar of ancient Chinese history, to accompany Ricardo so, as he told Ricardo, "You can fully grasp just how impressive this hidden treasure really is."

The site was a massive burial tomb built for the first emperor of China, Qin Shi Huang, more than fifteen hundred years earlier. Emperor Qin wanted to live forever, and he searched his entire life for the elixir of life and immortality. Emperor Qin created a huge army to keep him in power in the afterlife.

Bin explained to Ricardo that 700,000 workers toiled for more than forty years on Emperor Qin's mausoleum. After some man-made and natural disasters, the Terra Cotta Army was ordered closed and buried. Its secret location, however, was passed down from emperor to emperor over the centuries.

The army consisted of eight thousand life-size statues buried with the emperor, of which no two soldiers were alike. The statues were different heights and each soldier wore different clothing. Men from the cavalry were dressed differently from those in the infantry. Even facial expressions varied – some soldiers looked tense and ready for battle, while others appeared happy and proud, like conquerors. Along with the army of soldiers were statues of hundreds of horses and chariots.

All of the soldiers held real weapons. Some had swords, spears and daggers, while others carried crossbows and arrows. To make the statues appear even more lifelike, they were coated in colorless lacquer and painted.

"What is terra cotta?" Ricardo asked Bin. "And who built these statues?"

"Terra cotta is a hard-baked clay," Bin explained. "Artists shaped the wet clay in a mold, dried it in the sun, and later baked it in a hot kiln to harden the clay."

"In 221 B.C., the King of Qin, Ying Zheng, united much of China after a war of 250 years. The king changed his title to Qin Shihuangdi, which means 'Divine August Emperor of Qin.' The emperor was an energetic visionary. During his reign, he conscripted armies to build roads and canals, as well as our Great Wall. He established a Chinese currency, standardized weights and measures, and made everyone in China write in one standard script instead of the numerous regional variations in use at the time. In my estimation, Emperor Qin was worthy of this great burial site."

When Ricardo returned to the palace, the emperor asked him what he thought of the Terra Cotta Army.

"To me, the army exemplifies the essence of China," Ricardo answered. "It was made with enormous effort, creativity and pride and is beautiful, moving and totally memorable. I loved it as I love all of China, Your Excellency."

Ricardo's answer pleased the emperor greatly.

Chapter Thirty-One
The Great Wall of China

he following week, Bin Li Wei took Ricardo on a tour of the Great Wall of China.

"Our first emperor, Qin Shi Huang, began building the wall to keep out invaders from the north, especially the Mongols. The wall was built out of stone and dirt by criminals, slaves and peasants under the oppressive supervision of the military. Millions worked on the wall, and hundreds of thousands died in the process. Many of them were simply buried under the wall. Its builders called it 'the longest cemetery on earth.'

"There are many legends about the Great Wall. One is

the story of Meng Jiangnus. Meng's husband died building the wall, and she went to the wall every day to mourn his passing. Her tears were so bitter that when they fell, a section of the wall collapsed and revealed her husband's skeleton. Meng then collected the bones and took them home for a proper burial."

As Bin and Ricardo walked past the many watchtowers, beacon signal towers, and blockhouses where the soldiers lived, Ricardo saw a group of soldiers standing on top of the tallest beacon tower.

"What is happening up there, Bin?"

"They are playing a crazy game called 'vine jumping.' They say it came from islanders in the South Pacific. Young men would try to prove their bravery by jumping off high towers head first, held only by vines attached to their ankles."

"Let's join them, Bin," Ricardo said excitedly.

"The emperor would surely have me killed if I let you jump from such a height," Bin replied.

"Tell him you could not catch me," Ricardo said as he

ran to the tower and started climbing.

At the top, the soldiers gladly tied vines to each of Ricardo's ankles and asked him how deep into the moat he wanted to go. "Do you want to have just your fingers touch the water, have your shoulders touch or do you want to go all the way under?" they asked.

Ricardo looked down into the moat and got a lump in his throat. He had not realized how far the drop from the tower to the water really was.

"All the way is the only way!" he yelled. Ricardo felt as though he was floating in air for the first few seconds, then he saw the water coming up to meet him. He landed with an enormous splash.

Ricardo jumped out of the water, raised his arms to the sky and let out a loud yell of excitement and joy. "Yaaah!"

On the way back to Dadu, Ricardo thanked Bin for taking him to the Great Wall. "That was an experience I will always remember."

"Would you jump again, Ricardo?" asked Bin.

"Not a chance, Bin. Not a chance."

Chapter Thirty-Two

The Chinese Museum of Culture

he next afternoon, the emperor invited Ricardo for tea. "Ricardo, I'd like you to accompany me to our Chinese Museum of Culture. This will give you a greater understanding of our country, our history and our people."

Ricardo followed the emperor through the palace halls until they reached doors leading to an enormous garden. He was invited to step into a golden litter carrier, called a *jiao*. The jiao was carried on the shoulders of four strong bearers. As they moved smoothly through the garden, Ricardo saw thousands of beautiful plants, trees and flowers, all neatly arranged in a most artistic manner. He was particularly impressed by the hundreds of yew and holly topiary trees trimmed in the shape of animals and people. There were birds, fish, cats and dogs, as well as monkeys, lions, tigers, camels, elephants and even a pair of whales.

The procession stopped in front of a large ornate building with colorful flower patterns cut into wooden pillars, a glazed orange tile roof, and stone carvings all around. As they stepped inside, Ricardo was impressed by the marble floors and walls, the beautiful courtyard and the exquisite wall paintings and statues throughout.

The emperor proudly told Ricardo, "I personally designed this museum. It is divided into three main chambers. The first room tells the history of our people, from our beginnings to today. The next room is dedicated to our Chinese arts, including music, painting, theater, poetry and literature. Let us stop here for a moment and listen to our musicians play some of our ancient Chinese instruments."

Ricardo found the music soothing and beautiful.

"As we proceed into the third chamber, you will see examples of discoveries and inventions made in China," the emperor continued.

Each chamber had its own curator, who gave the emperor and Ricardo a private tour. Their knowledge was vast, and they answered the many questions Ricardo pressed upon them thoroughly and without hesitation.

While each of the presentations was mesmerizing, Ricardo was particularly intrigued by the chamber of Chinese inventions and discoveries. In the few months since his arrival in China, Ricardo had been able to get a feel for Chinese ingenuity, determination and love of beauty. However, he had no idea about the long history of contributions the Chinese people had made to the world.

The curator began telling Ricardo about China's most significant inventions: the compass, gunpowder, paper-making and printing, each offering a unique impact on the world. Then, in rapid order, the curator listed even more: the dripping water mechanical clock and the earthquake detector. Ricardo was amazed to learn that the umbrella and porcelain were invented in China almost three thousand years ago, and bronze for tools and weapons actually came over one hundred years before that. Alcohol, called *jiu* in Chinese, was first used for spiritual offerings to heaven and earth ancestors. The abacus, the crossbow and the hot air balloon were also developed by the ancient Chinese, along with matches, iron smelting and stirrups for riding horseback.

"Could all this be possible?" Ricardo thought to himself. "Are they taking credit for inventions from other countries as well as their own?" But the documentation about even the simplest inventions – like the toothbrush, chopsticks and the kite – was quite thorough. And the Chinese also invented ice cream, a delicacy Ricardo had yet to taste.

Ricardo was having trouble absorbing all of this incredible information when the curator began to describe how the Chinese invented the process of making silk from the cocoons of silkworms, then kept this process a secret from the rest of the world for hundreds of years. The curator also explained that paper money and a sophisticated postal service had come from Chinese ingenuity.

As expected, the section devoted to health was of particular interest to Ricardo. The Chinese had been using curative herbs for centuries. They invented acupuncture and had long been proponents of healthy eating, exercise and getting plenty of rest as the keys to a long life.

Other achievements highlighted in the museum were the first concept of decimal numbers and Pi, the first encyclopedia, and a written history that went back thousands of years. There was an original copy of Sun Tzu's *The Art of War*, which had been the primer for military strategists for centuries. The tour ended with models of China's archeological and engineering feats, including the Great Wall of China, the Silk Road trade route, the Grand Canal, and the Dali Pagodas.

By the tour's end, Ricardo was completely exhausted.

When the bearers realized Ricardo had fallen asleep the minute he climbed back into his jiao, they walked slowly and softly back to the palace. The emperor ordered his servants to gently carry Ricardo to a guest room. When Ricardo woke the next morning, he was wearing a pair of fine silk pajamas.

Chapter Thirty-Three
The Chinese New Year

The emperor spoke to Ricardo. "Tonight is the evening before our Chinese New Year festival. Join us for our reunion dinner. It is called *Nian Ye Fan* based on the following legend.

"The story goes that a mythical beast called Nian ate villagers, especially children. One year, as all the villagers hid from the beast, an old man stayed to face him. The old man put red papers up on the village windows and set off firecrackers all through the night. Nian was afraid and ran into the hills, never to be seen again. Because of this, it is a tradition for our people to wear red clothes and hang red lanterns on their doors and windows every year at this time."

When the emperor explained that it was customary for families to carefully clean their houses to 'sweep away bad fortune and allow good luck to enter,' it reminded Ricardo of how his grandmother used to sweep all bread from their home once a year at Passover.

At dinner that evening, Bin sat next to Ricardo and explained how the Chinese New Year is a time for families to honor ancestors and deities. "Since eight is a lucky number in China, eight individual dishes are served. It is also traditional to serve *jaozi* dumplings, which we will eat later in the evening.

"The highlight of the dinner for me is *niangao*, a wonderful dessert known as Chinese New Year pudding. It signifies a more prosperous year ahead. I love it."

As Ricardo and Bin were enjoying their niangao, the chef brought over a special bowl covered with glass. "We made this for you, Ricardo, on orders from our emperor." The chef removed the covering and proudly revealed his offering.

"What is it?" Ricardo asked incredulously.

"Ice cream. It is made with snow from the mountains, rice and fresh fruit. We hope you like it."

Ricardo loved it. It tasted cool, refreshing and delicious. He was moved by the emperor's thoughtfulness and that he remembered Ricardo had never tasted ice cream before.

After dessert, the emperor came to each of the guests and handed them a red envelope. Ricardo's was filled with Chao, Chinese currency. He also gave Ricardo a string of copper coins. This was more money than Ricardo had ever seen.

Just then, Ricardo heard a huge bang and the sky seemed to explode as a spectacular fireworks display began.

"How do they do that, Bin?"

Bin told him that hundreds of years ago, Chinese scientists mixed sulfur, charcoal and saltpeter to make gunpowder.

"It was used only for fireworks for many years," Bin explained, "until Chinese inventors discovered they could use the mixture to make weapons. First, they made fire arrows, but much later gunpowder became the explosive ingredient in cannons. I am afraid that gunpowder will be a danger and a curse to our future generations, Ricardo."

Later that night, as he was falling asleep, Ricardo reflected on his evening – the eight-course dinner, the ice cream dessert, the emperor's gift of money, and the awe inspiring fireworks.

"China is a fascinating country," he thought as he drifted to sleep, "but I hope Bin's fears about gunpowder are wrong."

Chapter Thirty-Four
Chinese Medicine
And
Acupuncture

uring the months Ricardo spent in China, he grew very close to Doctor Jai-Guo, who was more than willing to be Ricardo's mentor and teacher of Chinese medicine and acupuncture.

Along with serving as the emperor's personal physician, Jai-Guo taught at the prestigious Dadu College of Medicine. Ricardo attended his lectures and met with him after each class to clarify what he didn't understand.

Jai-Guo explained that, for more than a thousand years, Chinese emperors were constantly searching for immortality, and this search for the *elixir of life* led to the discovery of many new remedies and medicines.

"Good health," Jai-Guo explained, "is based on the Tao-ist philosophy that all phenomena are composed of two opposite yet interconnected forces, called *yin* and *yang*. These forces combine to form a person's life force, or *qi*. Traditional Chinese medicine teaches that disease is caused by yin and yang being out of balance in one's body."

Ricardo listened carefully as Jai-Guo explained that Chinese physicians believed that the path to harmony and good health can be advanced through acupuncture, or *zhenjiu*, and by using herbal medicines. Zhenjiu treats patients by the inserting and manipulating of needles in the body in an effort to balance the body's qi.

"I will be happy to teach you, Ricardo. Let's start by having you understand how it feels to have needles put in you."

Jai-Gou took out a leather case with dozens of needles of different lengths and thicknesses. Some were as thin as a piece of silk thread.

Ricardo felt no discomfort until needles were placed inside his ears and he felt a sharp pinching sensation.

The next day, Jai-Gou introduced Ricardo to a heat treatment. He placed needles into his arms and legs and burned the herb *mugwort* at each needle point.

"The heat through the needle will chase the *black dragon spirit* out of your body, Ricardo."

Ricardo became Jai-Gou's most dedicated student of Zhenjiu, and soon Jai-Gou was allowing his student to insert and manipulate needles on his own patients. Jai-Gou told Ricardo he had a natural talent for acupuncture and should bring the art back with him to Madrid.

During their many hours together, Jai-Gou and Ricardo often discussed the differences between remedies for medical conditions in the West versus the East.

"Along with zhenjiu, we prescribe *ginseng weed, cow's stomach* and *sheep's eye* for depression," said the doctor.

"And we recommend *St. John's Wort and saffron extract, along with exercise and rest*," countered Ricardo.

"We treat fever with *catnip, lavender* and cold compresses," Ricardo continued. "We also use *cayenne pepper* and *elderflower tea* to make the patients sweat."

"In China," Jai-Gou replied, "along with zhenjiu, we use ginseng and *menthol* extract, *yarrow* tea, to treat fever. We also use a *mustard* foot bath to ease the fever by drawing blood to the patient's feet."

Both Jai-Gou and Ricardo were pleased to learn that when it came to colds, flu and other ailments, Western and Eastern remedies were quite similar. Only their Latin or Chinese names differed.

When Ricardo's education in Chinese medicine ended, Jai-Guo gave him a set of zhenjiu needles with a note that read:

To Ricardo,
My student and friend,
Jai-Guo

Chapter Thirty-Five
Mongolia

The emperor invited Ricardo to join his royal court at a Mongolian sports festival in Xanadu. Ricardo thought Xanadu was the name of a fantasy city when he first saw it on his map. "It is just three day's travel on the other side of the Great Wall," the emperor told Ricardo. "From there, it will be easy for you to pick up our *Yam postal route* and visit major cities on the *Silk Road* on your way back to Europe and your family."

Ricardo learned much about Mongolia and its people from the emperor during the three-day trip. "We have a proud history," the emperor told him. "Ancient legend has it that Grey Wolf and Beautiful Deer joined together to create the Mongolian people. Mongolia was inhabited by tribal people for many centuries until we were unified under the powerful leader Genghis Khan, the *Universal Ruler* who, though often brutal, was a military genius. Because we Mongols are great warriors, Genghis Khan and his armies controlled much of the world as we know it. The Mongol horsemen were able to move at speeds much greater than their enemies. For example, during an attack they often did not stop for nourishment. Instead, they nicked a vein in their horse's neck and drank the blood in order to keep moving forward. Genghis Kahn's grandson was my grandfather, the great Kublai Khan, the founder of our Yuan Dynasty in China."

The emperor continued, "We are a nomadic, pastoral people. Because of the harsh climate, we have little tillable soil, so our survival depends on products from our grazing animals – cattle, camels, horses, sheep and goats. We eat mostly soups, dumplings, cooked meats and dairy products. After we took over China, we added noodles and rice to our diet. We cook with fires fed by dried animal dung. Our families live in *gers*, portable dwellings. When our herds eat up the grass, we pack up our gers and move to fresh pastures."

The emperor told Ricardo about a festival called *Naadam*, which featured archery, wrestling, horse racing and a traditional *buzkashi* contest. Buzkashi literally means "goat pulling," and the object of this violent and dangerous sport is to place a goat carcass in a goal.

"It is like your futbol on horseback, but without many rules."

When the emperor and Ricardo arrived at the festival, thousands of people had already gathered. It began with an elaborate ceremony, which included the presentation of nine tails from Genghis Khan's horses. This was followed by men, women and children in native costumes singing traditional Mongolian songs. Next, a parade of eagle hunters on horseback put on a display showcasing the speed and agility of their birds, along with their own horsemanship. It was all very exciting to Ricardo.

Merchants at the festival sold fermented mare's milk called *airag* and steamed dumplings called *buuz*, which were filled with ground beef – often horse meat.

Earlier, when Ricardo had told the emperor about his experience in Africa, and he mentioned his training in martial arts with the chief's finest warriors. "I remember hearing of your experience with the warriors in Africa," said the emperor, "so I thought it would be great fun for you to test your skills today and tomorrow. You are signed up in all three of the sports: archery, wrestling and horse racing."

"That is very kind of you, Great Emperor," Ricardo replied, "but it has been many months since I shot an arrow, wrestled or raced a horse." The emperor gave Ricardo a look that clearly communicated that he expected his wishes to be followed without question, and soon Ricardo was standing with a bow in his hand in a row of archers. The targets were placed at four distances, starting at one hundred *chi* and increasing to the seemingly impossible distance of five-hundred chi. Each archer was given four arrows for each distance. Because he was a guest participant, Ricardo was also allowed to shoot three practice arrows at each distance. Remembering his warrior training, Ricardo forced himself to relax by slowing down his breathing and thought of Chief Hin's instructions to "focus, inhale, slowly exhale and release." After his practice arrows all hit their targets, Ricardo gained confidence and was ready to compete. To the surprise of the crowd and the emperor in particular, most of Ricardo's arrows were true, and he was one of three archers remaining in the competition as they stood in front of the farthest targets.

Ricardo's practice arrows all fell short of the target, so on his first official attempt he raised his bow slightly...and his arrow hit the target a bit below the bull's-eye. Ricardo's next two arrows struck close to center and his last was a perfect, dead-center hit. The next finalist scored a little better than Ricardo and the last archer – who happened to be the Mongolian national champion – put all of his arrows in the center of his target. There were cheers from the crowd for all three finalists, and although Ricardo finished third, he was quite pleased with his performance. The emperor came over and complimented Ricardo on his skills, "But now I want to see you wrestle."

Ricardo soon learned that wrestling was the most popular sport in Mongolia. Children wrestled competitively and were taught from a very early age to fight wisely and hard. Wrestlers were paired by weight, and each bout continued until one of them was pinned to the ground for fifteen seconds or conceded defeat.

For his size and weight, Ricardo was quite strong. He also knew some effective moves from his warrior training and was not the least bit afraid. He easily defeated his first four opponents, then faced a skilled and clever Turkic fighter. Their match continued for more than an hour until Ricardo's opponent pinned him down and held his shoulders to the ground for the required fifteen seconds. Both combatants were totally exhausted when it was over. The victorious Turkic fighter helped Ricardo to his feet and they hugged out of respect for each other's strength and determination.

The next day was devoted to horse racing. Young boys and girls raced short distances on their horses, but the main event was a thirty-two kilometer cross-county race over hills ending in a stretch of desert. Almost all of the riders were men in their twenties and thirties who were either ranchers or soldiers. Then there was Ricardo, who was given a feisty brown stallion to ride.

"His name is Bataar," the horse's handler told him. "It means 'hero.'" When they led the horse to Ricardo it reared up, and when they tried to saddle him, the horse fought and kicked wildly. Ricardo walked up to Bataar and began softly singing to him. The melody that came to mind was the one he had taught Armoldo, set to the Spanish nursery rhyme *Asserrin, Asserran*:

My name is Bataar, a Mongol warrior you see

I run like the wind, you cannot catch me

My name is Bataar, my spirit is free

I am a hero, try and catch me.

Within a few moments, Ricardo had his arms around Bataar's neck as he rubbed his coat. He put his face next to Bataar's and felt a sweet connection, similar to the one he felt with Kelen back in the Sahara. Ricardo was blessed with a love for animals; the animals sensed that feeling and loved him back. He saddled Bataar and they moved to the starting line.

The rules of the race were simple: ride as fast as you can. The riders were required to collect colored flags placed in the sand every four kilometers. Ricardo's flags were purple to match his saddle blanket. Bataar was fast – very fast – and he loved to run. Ricardo and another horseman named Sukh broke away from the pack early, matching each other stride for stride. Ricardo was thinking what fun this race was when he felt the sting of Sukh's whip over and over against his back.

After his initial surprise and anger, Ricardo yelled, "Let's win this race, Bataar! Let's run like the wind!" And they did. Ricardo collected all eight of his flags far sooner than Sukh and was declared the winner. He was awarded three sheep for his victory, which he donated to the local orphanage.

Sukh, who was a member of the small Jewish community of Karakorum in Mongolia gave Ricardo a *Mazel Tov* for his victory and told him that he performed a *mitzvah*, or good deed, by giving the sheep to those who needed them the most.

That night, Ricardo attended the emperor's banquet, where he was toasted by all of the competitors of Nadaam, including Sukh.

All watched as the judges beheaded and disemboweled a goat, cut off its two hind legs, and soaked it in water to toughen it. What was left of that poor goat was to be the object of Buzkhasi the next morning.

When they arrived at the event, the emperor told Ricardo that he had also signed him up for the Buzkhasi tournament...then burst into laughter.

"I was only joking, my friend. You did yourself proud in battle these past two days. Why don't you just sit with me and relax as we watch the action?"

The competitors, ten men on each side, were dressed in heavy clothing to protect themselves from the others players' whips and boots as they fought to control the goat carcass. The aim was to grab it away from the opposing players, ride to the far goal, encircle a marker and throw the carcass into the scoring circle, called 'the circle of justice.' The competition was fierce, and even though the rules penalized players for whipping a rider intentionally or knocking him off of his mount, those transgressions happened all over the field. The emperor explained that some Buzkashi matches last for two days. This one, however, lasted only five hours since one team was so much stronger than the other and reached the required fifteen goals with relative ease.

"What a memorable way to leave Asia," Ricardo thought. "I saw and learned so much. Mostly, I hope to return here one day."

The emperor said goodbye to Ricardo with a gentle hug, four gifts and a request.

The first gift was a ruby and gold bracelet for Ricardo's mother. In its box was a note in Mongolian that read, "You blessed the world with a fine son."

The second gift was a *paiza*, a Mongolian passport for travel along the Yam system until Ricardo reached Istanbul. The gold-engraved passport guaranteed food, a bed and remounts at hundreds of postal relay stations from China all the way to Europe. Ordinarily, this pass was given only to emissaries and ambassadors, but it would help guarantee Ricardo safe passage, most of the way back to Spain. To be certain Ricardo was protected on his journey, the emperor also dispatched four horse archers as bodyguards.

"Ricardo, your third gift is Bataar. I know you will treat him as family."

The emperor's last gift was an intricately carved jeweled statue of a dragon, the Chinese and Mongol symbol of strength, power and good luck. Tradition dictated that these statues were only given to those who were honorable and worthy.

The emperor's request was that Ricardo be his emissary and, in that capacity, deliver to Pope Innocent VI a letter and a gift, a jeweled statue matching the one he gave Ricardo, in honor of his inauguration as head of the Catholic Church. Ricardo was honored to grant the emperor's request, especially after witnessing the emperor's generosity and hospitality over the past several months. And Ricardo had another thought of why he was happy to deliver the emperor's letter and gift.

"This gives me a wonderful reason to visit Rome."

THE JOURNEY HOME

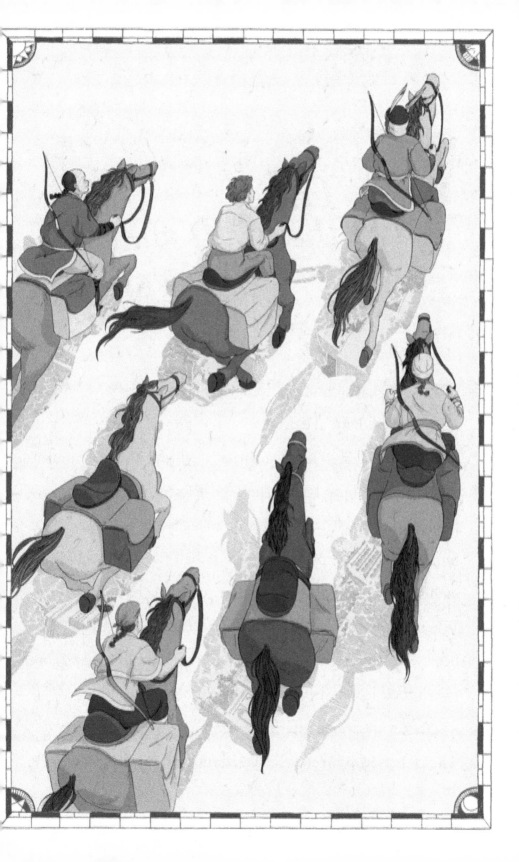

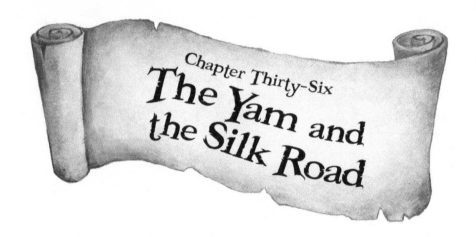

Chapter Thirty-Six
The Yam and the Silk Road

icardo and his four young horse-archer escorts — Arban, the leader of the group, Feng, Tae and Takai — left Xanadu at daybreak the next morning. The four boys barely spoke to Ricardo for the first few hours, until they took a break to eat and to water their horses. Then, Tae pulled a cowhide ball filled with sand out of his pocket and the four began to toss it back and forth. When the ball came to Ricardo, he eagerly joined in. The boys were quite agile, and caught the ball with one hand, between their legs and even over their shoulders.

Arban described the route they were taking to Ricardo. Their first stop would be Lanzhou, followed by Kashgar,

Osh, Bahlika, Bukhara, Merv, Hamadēn, Antioch and Constantinople – each of the cities was marked on the map as
part of the Silk Road. The escorts would leave Ricardo in
Rome after the letter and gift were delivered to the pope.
The journey to Rome was over nine thousand kilometers,
and then Ricardo would travel another two thousand kilometers from Rome back home to Madrid. Arban estimated
the trip to Rome would take two months if they changed to
fresh horses at every relay stop on the Yam. Ricardo asked,
"What will I do with Bataar? The emperor instructed me to
treat him as family."

"He is a strong stallion, Ricardo." Arban replied. "If we
bring two extra horses with us, you could alternate riding
them with Bataar. If you only ride Bataar a few hours each
day that would make the trip much easier for him and will
only add a few weeks to our journey.

We will sleep at the relay stations whenever we can, and
in our sleeping bags out in the open air when we must.
When we arrive at major cities on the Silk Road to resupply
– like Kashgar and Constantinople – we will rest and let you

enjoy the sights for a few days."

"Will there be time for fun and adventure along the way, Arban?" asked Ricardo.

"Of course, "Arban responded, "especially if it involves tests of courage. We four like to challenge each other. We are friends, but we love to compete. You can join our contests any time you wish."

Their first stop, Lanzhou, was a center for trade on the Silk Road in northwest China. Lanzhou was beautiful, with mountains to the north and south and the Yellow River running through the heart of the city. Feng, the scholar of the group, proudly explained to Ricardo that the Mongols captured the city in 1235 and named it *Jin Cheng*, the Gold City, because of the Silk Road trading that was done there.

The boys, with their horses, set up camp in a park on the banks of the river. The four escorts raced each other in the river until they realized Ricardo did not know how to swim very well. Ricardo was a quick learner though, and soon he stroked through the water with ease. There was a tree overhanging the riverbank with a rope tied to a limb about half-way up. The boys climbed the tree, shimmied out on the limb, grabbed the rope and swung out, then let go, landing with a large splash. Takai said, "Watch me, fellows."

Takai climbed past the limb, past the green canopy to the very top of the tree where he carefully moved hand over hand until he reached the tree's edge. Then he jumped, making a huge splash. The boys cheered as they waited for Takai to surface. They waited and waited, until finally Arban dove into the water to search for his friend. "He is not there!" Arban yelled. "Where can he be?"

Just then, they heard a laugh downstream. It was Takai. After his jump, he held his breath and swam along the bottom just to scare his companions. It worked! However, Takai cut his leg on the tree branches and the wound was beginning to hurt. Ricardo opened his medical pack, washed out the cut and mixed together *thyme* and blackberries. Spying an *Adler tree*, he stripped off some bark and ground it with the other ingredients into a paste. He applied white vinegar to Takai's cut, followed by the paste. He soothed it with aloe and wrapped it in a piece of cloth. By the next morning, the cut was nearly healed.

Ricardo preferred camping on the road or in a relay station over staying in the cities. He enjoyed the freedom of physical activities with his new friends as they wrestled, raced their horses and, of course, threw the ball.

In Kashgar, Ricardo showed the authorities his paiza, and the group was completely resupplied, including food for their horses. This hospitality reminded Ricardo of the power and reach of the Khans and the Yuan Dynasty.

Their little caravan advanced toward Osh. The highlight in the city of Osh was the food, and the boys decided to rest their horses and linger for a few days in this hospitable place. At the Jayma Bazaar, the boys engaged with merchants of all backgrounds, trading exquisite textiles, pottery, silks and gold in the narrow alleys of the city. Wherever the boys went in Osh, they were welcomed warmly, often with delicious local fare. The Mongol boys especially loved nomadic foods like *Osh plov*, made with red rice, meat, vegetables and spices. There was *maida Manti*, handmade dumplings filled with mashed potatoes, and *mega-samsa*, flaky dough pastries filled with lamb and onions, cooked to perfection in a tandoor oven with chili peppers and covered with sesame seeds.

The travelers were in heaven! And then there was the bread, especially the *lepyoshka* bread, baked in a special oven. The aromas provided a warm welcome to any one regardless of background. No one seemed to argue or fight in Osh. Perhaps, Ricardo thought, the delightful food aromas elevated people's moods. After three days of glorious eating, the boys reluctantly returned to the road.

On the way to Bahlika, Ricardo taught his companions the Qadamy game he and Martim made up in the desert. Although they caught on quickly, they were bored of it within a few days.

"We are Mongols," Tae said. "We are horse people. Let's play these games on our horses! I wonder if we can create something that is light enough to be thrown or shot long distances that we can chase it down with our mounts?"

No one had any immediate ideas.

"Maybe we will be inspired as we ride further along the Silk Road," suggested Tae. But inspiration never came.

In Bahlika, there was a museum with a large number of Sanskrit medical and pharmaceutical texts. Ricardo spent time with the curator of the museum and proudly showed him his father's journal. Ricardo's companions were quite impressed with his knowledge of medicinal plants and remedies, but holding that journal made Ricardo wonder how his father was feeling. He hoped his family was thinking about him as much as he thought about them.

Tae was preoccupied with creating a game they could play while mounted on their horses. He recalled how the flat breads of Osh were taken out of the ovens and flipped to servers across the restaurants, and that gave him an idea.

"Why not make a flat piece of wood that we can sail to each other while riding?"

"That will be too heavy," replied Arban, "but what if it was made of bird carcasses? The bones are hollow and very lightweight. They can be pressed and glued into shape, perhaps like a bird with its wings outstretched in flight."

"It won't fly far enough if we just threw it," Tae responded, "but what if we shot it from a small crossbow?"

"We would need to add a small weight in the front to help it fly farther," added Feng. "It just might work."

On their way to Bukhara, the next city on the Silk Road, the boys drew diagrams and picked up bird carcasses that they crushed, shaped and glued until they had several prototypes of their "flying bone."

To test their product, the boys climbed to the top of the Bukhara's Kalyan Minaret, also known as the *Tower of Death*. It had earned that nickname over the centuries as a place where criminals were thrown off the top to be executed. After several of their models failed to fly, the boys were elated when one sailed far when they shot it out of the crossbow, then fell gracefully to the ground.

They coated the successful model in lacquer and painted it red, then flew it back and forth between them as they rode on to Merv. They dubbed it the "Silk Road Flyer." It wasn't perfect, but it worked. Most importantly, it was fun!

Arban told the boys that Merv was once called *queen of the cities*, which only one hundred years earlier had been the world's largest city. He explained, "The city was built on top of an oasis, in the middle of a busy trade route. The people from Merv were mostly prosperous and educated. The city was a center of learning for Buddhists and Muslims and the home to famous poets, scientists, physicians and scholars. In the year 1221, the ruling sultan defied an order to "surrender or die" from Genghis Khan and his son Tolui. The Kahns attacked and destroyed the dam feeding the oasis, and killed more than 700,000 inhabitants. The city never fully recovered from this disaster." Arban continued, "Since it borders on so many countries on the Silk Road, Merv is still a minor center for commerce." Merv was once a crossroads of ideas, inventions and cultures. Sadly, today the city has become a crossroads for disease, since the plague traveled through Merv on its path of death. Ricardo told his companions about his father's terrible dance with death from the plague. After a short discussion, the boys decided not to visit Merv.

Instead, they traveled west for many days until they reached the ancient city of Hamadēn. At the entrance to the city, they were met by a number of local guides, each who tried to convince the boys to hire them for tours of the well known area attractions: the *Ali Sadr Cave*, the *Tomb of Avienna* and the *Tomb of Esther and Mordechai.*

Arban, acting as the leader, asserted, "we have not yet relied on guides in our journey, why start now?" One of the guides cautioned, "many travelers have disappeared in the dangerous waters of the Ali Sadr Cave. You need someone with knowledge of the cave to lead you through it safely. I, Farrakh, will be your navigator, and at the end of the day, you can pay me whatever you feel my guidance was worth."

"That seems quite fair. We accept your offer," answered Arban. "Lead on please."

During the long ride to the north, Farrakh explained that he was a Zoroastrian and that his name meant "a happy and fortunate man."

Feng timidly asked Farrakh to tell them about Zoroastrianism.

"In simple terms, Zoroastrianism is one of the world's oldest religions. Our faith was founded by the Prophet Zoroaster in ancient Iran more two thousand years ago. We believe in one god, *Ahura Mazda*, our creator, and regard life as a battle between good and evil. We believe that, in the end, evil will be destroyed."

"What religion are you, boys?" Farrakh asked.

"The four of us are from Mongolia. We are proud that our people practice many beliefs and are accepting of all religions," responded Takai. Arban and I are Buddhists, Tae is an Islamist and Feng... Feng, what is your religion?"

"I practice Shamanism," explained Feng. "We believe in a direct connection between man and nature and that we are intermediaries between our world and the spirit world. We are personally responsible to our community, our family and to all creation."

Farrakh responded thoughtfully, "That sounds like a beautiful religion to me."

All the boys looked at Ricardo, waiting for his response.

"I am not certain what my religion is. My family attended church on major Catholic holidays like Easter and Christmas, but we did not practice religion in our home. I have some faint recollections of my grandparents celebrating Passover and other Jewish holidays, but I honestly am not sure. Several times since I left home I have felt strongly attached to the history and customs of the Jewish people, especially when I was in Jerusalem. When I stood at the Wall, I felt very close to God," Ricardo concluded.

Farrakh informed Ricardo that his family had a friendly relationship with Rabbi Yosef of Hamadēn. He was certain that the Rabbi would love to meet Ricardo. "But first, let us enter the glorious Cave of Ali Sadr, a true wonder of the world!" exclaimed Farrakh.

Ali Sadr was a gigantic water cave that they entered on the side of a hill. Once inside, Farrakh offered a coin to a young boy who returned with a flat bottom boat and oars. They paddled through several large lakes fed by a river within the many chambers of the cave. Farrakh pointed out images of animals, bows and arrows and hunting scenes on the cave walls. Primitive man lived in the cave thousands of years ago.

The boys were captivated by the beauty inside the cave and by its enormity. "I can see how easy it would be to get lost in here, " observed Tae. "We were right to hire you, Farrakh."

Back in Hamadēn, Farrakh took the boys to meet Rabbi Yosef. The rabbi and his wife, Sarah, lived in simple quarters adjacent to the town's synagogue. Sarah insisted that the travelers be their guests while in Hamadēn, and immediately began to prepare dinner for them. She explained that it was Friday evening, their *Sabbath,* or *Shabbat,* and asked the boys, including Farrakh, to wash up to be ready to greet the Sabbath. They boys honored her wishes, and soon all eight of them were sitting together watching Sarah light candles. The Rabbi chanted blessings over the wine, the *Challah bread* and then the food began to appear. Ricardo wondered how Sarah was able to produce such delicious dishes from such a tiny, modest kitchen.

After a tasty chicken soup, there was *gondi nokhodchi,* (chicken meatballs), *gondi kashi,* (rice with turkey, fava beans, beets and herbs), and all served with warm Challah and wine. The meal was followed with a dessert of pistachio shortbread, dried apricots and a vanilla cardamom syrup. The Rabbi concluded the meal with additional blessings, thanking God for Shabbat for allowing all of them to be together on such a special day.

Early the next morning, Ricardo accompanied the rabbi to Shabbat prayer services. Rabbi Yosef wrapped Ricardo in a white *tallit* prayer shawl with fringes at each corner, and suggested he hum along with the congregants when they sang. Ricardo was quite moved by the experience.

At lunch, the Rabbi shared the Jewish history of Hamadēn with his guests.

"The city was first mentioned in the Book of Ezra as the place where a scroll was found that gave the Jews permission from King Darius to rebuild the temple in Jerusalem."

Rabbi Yosef then proudly told the boys the following story.

"When the temple was destroyed in Jerusalem, the Jewish people were forced to flee to other lands, including Persia. King Ahasuerus of Persia chose the beautiful young Jewish woman, Esther, as his bride. Esther's uncle Mordechai had previously saved the king by exposing an assassination plot against him. A wicked man named Haman was a key advisor to Ahasuerus and when Mordechai refused to bow to him, Haman declared that Mordechai and all the Jews in the Persian Empire must die. He even built a gallows for the hanging of the Jews. Mordechai discovered Hamen's terrible plans, and exhorted Esther to speak to the king.

This meant revealing herself to be a Jewess and begging for the king's mercy on her people. King Ahasuerus loved Esther and remembered the kindness Mordechai had shown him years earlier. He declared that Haman should be the one to die by hanging, and that the Jewish people should live safely in his country. Esther became a heroine to our people who celebrate the holiday called Purim to honor her for saving our Jewish people."

"I like the story of Purim, Rabbi," exclaimed Farrakh, "not as much as I love the Passover story, but it grows on me every time I hear you tell it."

Rabbi Yosef chuckled at Farrakh's honesty.

"Ricardo, there is one other place in our city that you must see, especially because of your interest in medicine," the Rabbi said. "It is called the Tomb of Avicenna *(Abn*

Sina) and it holds the famous *Canon of Medicine,* a summary of all medical knowledge in the world at the time it was written around the year 1000." As they entered the tomb, they learned that Avicenna was the icon of medical knowledge in the Islamic world. He was exceptionally brilliant, had memorized the Quran by age ten and studied Euclid, Aristotle, law, and medicine as a teen. He wrote more than 450 books on subjects ranging from alchemy to physics to psychology. The curator of the Canon of Medicine generously allowed Ricardo to read the invaluable manuscript, and Ricardo pored through it long into the night. As he read, Ricardo felt a special kinship with his father who had instilled in him such a love and appreciation of medicine and healing.

There was a long farewell with Rabbi Yosef, Sarah and Farrakh. The Rabbi handed Ricardo a tallit. "This is so you will remember us and the long history of your Jewish people, Ricardo."

As they moved farther away from Hamadēn and traveled along the Silk Road toward Antioch, Ricardo began to think once again that he and his family might have Jewish roots.

Chapter Thirty-Seven
Antioch

rban informed his crew, "We have one more stop on our journey before arriving in Constantin-ople... Antioch."

"I studied Antioch in our history class in school," volunteered Feng. "I actually made a presentation about the city. Antioch has a very violent history. In fact, it may still be too dangerous for us to stop there.

"Antioch was founded in the fourth century B.C.E by Seleucus Nicator, one of Alexander the Great's generals, and became a strategic business and cultural center of the Roman Empire. Under Roman rule, building expanded around the city, with aqueducts, an amphitheater, improved roads adding to the landscape. Antioch grew and its people prospered."

Feng was correct about Antioch's history. The name "Christian" originated from Antioch. According to the New Testament, Peter and Paul preached there. As time went on, Antioch became the center of religious conflict, primarily between Muslims and Christians. In the Fourth Century under Constantine, Antioch was a leading city in the rise of Christianity, however when it was captured by the Turks and Tartars, Antioch was stained with Christian blood.

Often, with revenge on their minds, the Crusaders (Christian soldiers) were also heartless to the Muslims when they retook the city. No one was unaffected by the brutality.

Tae added, "What a harsh history. In a few hours, we will find out how the city is faring now."

The five boys soon discovered that Antioch was still suffering. On the outskirts of the city near a stream, they spied a makeshift camp of homeless and despondent people. Ricardo immediately noticed that there were few children to be seen.

A dignified gentleman dressed in fine, yet tattered clothes, stepped in their path as the boys approached.

"Welcome to Antioch. Unfortunately, we can't welcome you properly as we have no food to share. As you can see, we are barely able to survive in this hell hole unfit for human habitation."

The boys were stunned by the desperate scene before them.

"How did you come to be in this terrible situation?" asked Tae. "Where are your children?"

The gentleman responded, "My name is Eymen Kaya, Mayor of Antioch. I was forced to leave our city along with all adults over the age of twenty."

Takai asked, "How could such a thing happen? There must be quite a story here."

"Yes, there is," replied Eymen, "but first, could you spare some food for my wife and me? Please do not take it out in front of everyone here, or you may incite a riot. Follow me to my tent," he added.

Arban and his band followed the mayor as requested, and gave him some cheese and bread. The boys dismounted, watered their horses, and then sat on the ground in a circle around Mayor Kaya and his wife, Miray. They watched as Eymen and Miray devoured the food in seconds.

The mayor began, "Last month, the Antioch City Council expelled four young men from our city who were caught stealing treasures from the Art Museum. These thieves were soon joined outside of Antioch by eight other members of their gang. Unfortunately, before we arrested them they stole and hid a valuable ancient Chinese urn.

"Days later, Antioch was the target of dozens of fire arrows tipped with gunpowder. The gang had traded the urn for several barrels of the deadly explosives. The gunpowder was more violent than any fire, earthquake or weapon our citizens had ever seen. They were frightened and shaken.

"The gang soon returned to the gates of Antioch, led by a twenty-year-old street thug named Ahmet. He threatened, 'Citizens of Antioch, listen to me. We have stocks of explosives and intend to harm you, your families and your homes if you do not obey our commands. All people older than twenty must leave the city at dawn. Take your babies with you. Children over the age of eight must stay to join us as soldiers or work for us as slaves. The choice is yours.'

"The people cried out, 'Where will we go? How will we eat? Who will care for our sick, our elderly?'

"Ahmet coldly replied, 'That is no concern of ours. You expelled us out from Antioch, and now it is your turn to leave.'

"From out of his pocket, he pulled a bag with a fuse attached. He lit the fuse and threw it into the crowd, screaming, 'Be gone by dawn or you will be dead by noon!' There were screams from those injured by the blast, and shrieks from those faced with the terrible choice of leaving Antioch and their children behind or dying at the hands of these cruel criminals."

"How terrible!" Arban exclaimed.

The mayor continued, "Most of us left the city the next day in an attempt to save our children and our homes. Amid tearful goodbyes we promised that our families would soon be reunited. We walked here, to this spot, and stayed for the water. We have been camped here ever since."

Ricardo stood up and spoke to the group, "I learned about gunpowder when I was in China."

Feng added, "We are familiar with explosives from our service in the Mongolian Army."

Arban jumped to his feet and shouted excitedly, "And what is the one thing that takes the fear out of gunpowder?"

All five boys yelled at the same time, "Water!"

Arban exclaimed, "We will help you get your city back, Mayor Kaya! First we need a map of the city, with information about where Ahmet's guards are positioned and where the barrels of gunpowder are stored. Can you provide that to us?" he asked.

The mayor reported that he could enter the city through ancient tunnels under the walls and make contact with his teenage daughters, Elif and Ecrin. He was certain that they could do reconnaissance and make the map. He was right.

Arban organized all the able-bodied men and women into five teams, each to be led by either Ricardo, Tae, Feng,

Takai or himself. Each person carried a gourd filled with water, and together they comprised a small but mighty army. Under the cover of night, the teams marched toward Antioch, and at dawn quietly pounced on the unsuspecting guards. When a guard grabbed for his pouch of explosives, they soaked the pouch thoroughly, and then tied and bound the guard. The five teams took less than one hour to overtake every sentinel guarding the city walls.

Next, the teams descended into the tunnels and followed the map to reach the store of gunpowder. Ahmet and his men had unwisely left the storehouse unguarded.

With the boys leading the way, followed by the mayor and his citizens, the army marched to where Ahmet and his lieutenants were sleeping soundly. The criminals awoke when they felt water being poured onto their faces.

"You will have plenty of time for sleep when you are in jail," the Mayor told the criminals as they were led away with their hands tied behind their backs.

Ricardo instructed the Mayor and his followers to carry the barrels of gunpowder outside the city walls and light them on fire. What a fireworks display! The City Council then swiftly proclaimed that no explosives of any kind would be allowed in Antioch again.

Antioch's families were reunited, and the townspeople showed their gratitude for Arban, Tae, Takai, Feng and Ricardo through tears, hugs and cheers. Mayor Kaya gave each hero a key to the city to thank them for their brave actions. For several days after their victory, the boys rested in Antioch. Everywhere they went, they were followed by laughing children who were grateful to be back with their friends and families.

Chapter Thirty-Eight
Constantinople

he boys had been on the road for many weeks when they arrived in Constantinople. Feng, their "resident scholar," gave them a historical review before they entered the city.

"Constantinople was built in the year 330 by the Roman Emperor Constantine, who named it after himself. It is part of the Byzantium Empire. Most of Constantinople's inhabitants are Eastern Orthodox, and the official language is Greek. Constantinople has been the capital of the Roman-Byzantine Empire for more than a thousand years, withstanding many foreign invaders."

The boys stopped at the city gates and showed their passports. Ricardo asked the guard, "Who is the leader of your city now?"

"The present patriarch of Constantinople is Kallistos I."

Ricardo suggested they present themselves to the patriarch. Kallistos greeted them with warmth and curiosity, and invited them to a hearty lunch. He told the boys that the food in Constantinople was a fusion of ancient Roman and Greek culinary traditions with the spices and recipes gleaned from the many merchants who passed through on the Silk Road. "Because we are situated between two bodies of water, we are avid fish eaters," Kallistos told them. "We often season our food with *garum*, which is a fish sauce, as well as ginger and nutmeg. By the way, boys, we invented forks and spoons here in Constantinople. They were devised to help our Byzantine nobles from getting their long sleeves soiled in their soup. We also are famous for our high-quality wines," he stated proudly.

"Your Excellency," Ricardo began politely, "since you mentioned that Constantinople is nearly surrounded by water, you must know many sea captains in your port. Could you help us secure sea passage to Rome? We are quite tired from our months of hard travel over land, and we heard that with the right connections, we could make it to Rome by going through the Straits of Bosporus to the Aegean Sea, then into the Mediterranean."

"I can handle that for you, boys," the patriarch answered.

"There is one little issue," Ricardo added. "We need to bring our horses with us. Can you arrange to have them travel on the boat with us?"

"Consider it done!"

All five boys thanked the patriarch for his assistance.

Kallistos offered them a place to sleep and to care for their horses that night. As they were leaving, he called out to them.

"Remember to visit our city walls. They have saved our Empire from our enemies many times."

Chapter Thirty-Nine
The Voyage to Rome

ven with their Silk Road passport and assurances from the patriarch, getting passage from Constantinople to Rome turned was no simple matter. None of the sea captains wanted to take the horses on board their ships. It seemed there was a recent agreement among the captains not to allow animals on board because of manure. A local physician had warned about the spread of the plague across continents; one theory was that it was passed in animal feces.

Just when it looked as though the group would be taking the longer overland route, Tae came up with an idea. "What if we made a bag that would attach to the back of our saddles and catch the droppings before they hit the deck of the boat. We could collect it, throw it over board, and clean the bags afterwards."

"Let's call it a horse diaper," said Ricardo.

"Or we can call it a 'poop collector,'" joked Takai. The name stuck.

The boys went to a local leather craftsperson and, within a few days, they had eight made-to-order poop collectors. After a quick demonstration for the captain and his crew of the *Daphne*, an agreement was reached and they set sail for Rome, with horses in tow.

Within just a few hours, Bataar and another horse, Maga, began acting strange. They started to stagger. The motion of the boat made Ricardo so dizzy that he had to lie down in order not to faint.

"The horses are seasick," Ricardo said weakly. "Feng, would you please get my medical bag and take out some ginger, saffron flowers and alfalfa, along with the mortar and pestle?"

Feng did as his friend asked, then watched Ricardo grind the items together and mix them with water. Ricardo poured the mixture into the cup of his hands and motioned for Bataar to drink. After seven handfuls of the solution, Bataar seemed back to normal. Ricardo did the same for Maga, and she recovered quickly as well. Ricardo ate some licorice and ginger, and felt much better.

The water in the Aegean and Mediterranean Seas was calm, which allowed the crew of the Daphne to have time away from their normal duties. Since the crew was made up of young boys, free time meant playing sports and games on board. Challenges came from Ricardo, Arban, Feng, Tae and Takai. The crew introduced them to a game of ship futbol, which included kicking the ball as they swung from the main mast of the vessel. Ricardo, in turn, showed the sailors how to play Qadamy and a simple version of the *Silk Road flyer.*

In the evenings, Feng played chess against the Daphne's best players and always came out the winner. In just a matter of days, all of the boys became friends. It made no difference that Ricardo was Spanish, his friends were Mongolian and the crew came from cities and villages across Europe, Asia and Africa. Not one of the boys thought about the fact that their new group included four Shamanists, two Buddhists, two Muslims, one Eastern Orthodox, two Roman Catholics, one Zoroastrian, one Animist and, circumstances suggested, one Jew. They were all bonded by sport, the sea, shared experiences and their exuberant youth.

Chapter Forty
Rome

s they arrived in Rome, Ricardo and his travel companions washed their horse poop collectors for the last time, shared warm goodbyes with the crew and captain of the Daphne, and walked their horses onto the docks of Rome. An unwelcoming group of men greeted them with, "Hey, China boys. You can't come ashore unless you pay us a landing fee. It costs two *florin* for each person and one florin for each horse. You owe us seventeen coins!"

Ricardo bravely confronted the eight heavily tattooed bullies. "By what authority do you collect these fees?"

The leader of the pack, a particularly surly man who looked to be about thirty years old, replied, "By the authority of our fists and by the authority of these weapons," turning back his cloak to reveal a knife and sword.

"We are not looking for any trouble," Ricardo answered. "We have our paizas, our passports and we are bearing a letter and gift for his Excellency the Pope."

There was laughter from the crowd. "The pope? The pope? He hasn't been in Rome for years. You need to go to Avignon to see the pope!"

At that moment, Ricardo realized why Avignon was marked on the map.

"No matter, sir," he coolly replied. "All that the five of us have on us are the clothes on our backs and the gift for the pope. No matter where he is now, I doubt you want to risk stealing from the leader of the Church. He would not look kindly on you, I am certain."

The bully stepped aside, trying to save face by retorting sarcastically, "Have a nice trip to Avignon. It's in France, you know."

Ricardo and Arban asked their companions to wait in the shade with the horses while they looked around and figured out their next move.

The two boys stopped in a quiet park just a few streets from the docks and sat on a bench near a group of merchants and religious leaders who were involved in an animated discussion.

"These gang members are ruining our community," cried one of the men. "They demand protection money from us. If we don't pay them, they break our store windows and steal our merchandise. Last week, they broke an entire shelf of my finest pottery when I refused to pay them!"

"They threatened my daughter and me at our fruit stand," lamented another.

"Look how they treat the elderly, our parents and grandparents, it is shameful!" added a woman in the group.

Ricardo walked over and said, "Tell us what they do. Perhaps we can help in some way."

The woman explained, "Every Sunday morning for as long as we can remember our parents would meet in this park. It was shady and cool and was a way to share time with families and friends. Each Sunday was a large neighborhood picnic. The Catholics came after church. Their Jewish neighbors came a bit earlier and set up the food.

"About a month ago, this gang of tattooed thugs came to the park and told us they were the new neighborhood protection service. They forced each person to pay one florin for the right to stay in the park; otherwise, we would have to leave. Two of our older leaders stood up to them and were beaten. The police did not want to get involved. They told us it is a neighborhood problem. It seems rather hopeless!"

"Perhaps not," said Arban. "We also have met this gang of thugs. I have an idea."

On Sunday, at exactly two o'clock, the eight bullies approached the crowd, starting with the elderly Jews who were quietly sitting and reading their Hebrew newspapers.

"Give us our protection money, Jew," the gang leader shouted, expecting everyone in the park to hear and comply.

From behind the newspapers, came heavy sticks and lead pipes. Ricardo, Arban, Feng, Tae and Takai had dressed in traditional religious garb and had convinced other young boys and girls from the community to do the same. And they came out swinging! The melee lasted only a few minutes, but it was very decisive. The bullies were bruised and beaten and certain to never terrorize the neighborhood again.

Ricardo and the boys became instant heroes.

Marcello, the mayor of the neighborhood, offered the five heroes a tour of Rome. By the time the tour left the park, they were accompanied by forty children from the neighborhood. It was a noisy but joyous affair.

Marcello began with a little history. "Legend says that Romulus and his twin brother Remus were abandoned at birth, then found and raised by a she-wolf. When the twin boys grew up, they fought. Romulus killed his brother and declared himself the first ruler of Rome. The Romans became a powerful force in the world. They built a road network of fifty-three-thousand kilometers."

As Marcello led the group through the majesty of Rome, he described each site they visited.

"The Colosseum once held 80,000 spectators to watch

gladiator contests, animal hunts and executions. We are here at the Roman Forum, where senators heard speeches from great orators such as Cicero, Caesar and Augustus. The Arch of Titus celebrated the siege of Jerusalem and the destruction of the holy Temple in 70 A.D."

When he heard that, Ricardo immediately thought of the Jews praying at the Wall in Jerusalem.

Marcello explained the importance of the seven hills of Rome and the Tiber River, then finished his tour at the magnificent Pantheon. Feng asked Marcello why there were so many stray cats in and around the historic buildings.

"It is due to the *cat laws* of Rome. Our cats are allowed to live without disruption in the place they were born. They are a part of our tradition.

Another Roman tradition was food – and lots of it – such as *suppli*, a fried rice ball with ragu and mozzarella; *flora dizucca*, zucchini flowers stuffed with mozzarella and anchovies; and *baccala*, cod baked in egg butter. Ricardo and his companions washed down the delicious food with an abundance of wine. The boys stayed in Rome for three days, rarely leaving the dinner tables of their neighborhood hosts. They heard the toasts *Salute, Cin Cin* and *L'Chiam* often during their stay.

Chapter Forty-One
Avignon

icardo told Arban, Feng, Tae and Takai that they had done what their emperor had asked of them, which was to escort him to Rome, and that they should return to their families in Mongolia. "I have been on the road for almost two years and am confident that I can take care of myself between here and Madrid," he said in a serious and sincere voice. The boys refused his offer, and Arban spoke up.

"We are with you until you deliver our emperor's gift to the pope, and until we are certain you are safely on your way home. We do this not only because we were ordered by the emperor, but because you are our friend."

Ricardo knew it was pointless to argue, so he simply thanked them for their loyalty and friendship.

Once in Avignon, Pope Innocent VI was quite amused when Ricardo and his companions told him they had gone to Rome to deliver his gift from the emperor of China.

"The papacy moved from Rome in 1309. There have been five popes since then. I guess news travels rather slowly these days," he said with a loud guffaw.

The pope's court was soon laughing as well. After a moment's embarrassment, the boys joined in the laughter.

The pope was very pleased with the exquisite jewel-covered dragon statue they presented to him. He especially liked the note attached to it:

From one great ruler to another.

May your reign be one of peace and happiness.

Signed,

Emperor Huizong of the Yuan Dynasty

Over a dinner of quail and wine from the papal vineyards, Innocent told the boys that the papacy had fallen on difficult times.

"The plague, tensions between church leaders, and wars between France and England have created huge demands on my treasury. I have made reforms to economize, sold off art and property, and worked to end the war. It has been a stressful time for me. Your visit has certainly brightened my day. Thank you."

Ricardo gave a warm farewell to each of his friends, saying he would write to them, making certain each letter would be delivered via the Yam postal system. They each gave him a hug and placed their foreheads next to his in a sign of deep friendship.

Following their goodbyes, Arban, Feng, Tae and Takai went east while Ricardo and Bataar, headed west.

Chapter Forty-Two

On to Spain

s Ricardo crossed the medieval Pont Saint Benezet bridge, he heard children singing:

"On the bridge of Avignon
We're all dancing, we're all dancing
On the bridge of Avignon
We're all dancing round and round."

Ricardo and Bataar moved on to Nimes, where they rested at the Roman temple *Maison-Caree.* They walked across the Pont di Gard and saw the aqueduct, the amphitheater and toured Magne Tower, all built by the Romans years before. "What a peaceful and beautiful town," thought Ricardo.

After a few days of sleeping in barns and sharing meals with welcoming farmers, Ricardo and Bataar came to the French border town of Cerebère on the coast. Ricardo was invited to dinner by Madame and Monsieur Bernard, proprietors of the only inn in town. During the meal, they warned Ricardo about a potential problem he might face in Spain while trying to reach his family.

There were rumors that a war was about to start in Spain between Aragon in the east and Castile in the center of the country. Both armies were looking for recruits, and they'd heard that sometimes the armies would kidnap young men and force them into service.

"I would stay off the roads if I were you, Ricardo," warned Madame Bernard. "I will make you a basket of food that will last you for many days so you can sleep in the woods and avoid stopping where the soldiers might grab you."

"Thank you both for your warning and your kindness," replied Ricardo. "It makes me sad to hear that my countrymen are fighting each other."

"It is not the people, Ricardo, but their rulers," Monsieur Bernard replied. "It seems like it is always the rulers, my boy! In this case, the disagreement is between Peter IV of Aragon and Peter of Castile. People around here say it will be called *The War of the Two Peters.*"

"I will be careful," promised Ricardo.

Ricardo quietly crossed the border at Pontbou, Spain, at night so as not to be detected. He and Bataar slept and ate in the forests and fields during the day and cautiously walked the roads at night. Ricardo decided to bypass Barcelona completely and kept heading west, always avoiding people – especially soldiers. He smiled to himself noting that Barcelona was not marked on his map. How did the mapmaker in India know that he would not be stopping there?

Ricardo's excitement grew as he approached Guadalajara, since it was only hours from his home. Guadalajara was one of the places marked as a destination on his map, but Ricardo was anxious to see his family. To save a little time, he abandoned his pattern of moving only at night and rode Bataar into the city early in the morning. There, he was stopped by Capitan Cruz of the Castilian Army.

"I have orders to enlist all young men for our army," the captain said. "Follow me."

Ricardo showed the captain his gold paiza, telling him, "I have a passport from the emperor of China that allows me safe passage in all of Europe and Asia."

"This decision is above my rank," replied the captain. "It will be up to my commanding officer, General de Longa."

Ricardo was taken to the tower at Castillo de Zafra, where he was questioned by the general.

"I am General Alvaro de Longa. Why would you have a passport from the emperor of China? Are you of royal blood?"

"No sir, I am from Madrid, the son of a pharmacist and a teacher. I am certainly not royalty, but I have been traveling for two years and was fortunate to spend time with the emperor. Please allow me to continue on my journey home."

"We need young men like you for our upcoming fight against Peter IV of Aragon. You will just have to wait a few more years to see your family," the general stated firmly.

"But I would like to hear of your adventures. I have always wanted to visit India and China, but my military career prevented me from going."

Hoping for a miracle, Ricardo began telling his story to General de Longa. When he related that he was inspired to be an explorer by Mateo Vasquez, the general jumped out of his chair and yelled, "You know Vasquez the Spanish explorer?"

"Yes sir, I do. He lives with my family in Madrid."

"Our king has been trying to locate him. He is needed to bear witness in a court case involving Spain, Genoa and Portugal concerning *Islas Canarias*, which you might know as the Canary Islands."

HOME

Chapter Forty-Three

Home

icardo and Bataar walked behind General de Longa and his twenty horsemen all the way to Madrid. As they entered the street where his family lived, Ricardo had a thought that made him chuckle.

"They could really use my 'poop collector' here."

The procession stopped in front of the Columbo family's apartment building. Two drummers and a trumpeter stepped forward, playing a military tune to announce their presence.

People rushed out from the neighborhood buildings to see what was happening. Some hid their teenage sons for fear they would be taken for military service.

Esteban and Anna were the first to see Ricardo. They screamed and ran to him. Next came Marta. Tears flowed freely over her flushed cheeks.

Alberto and Mateo came out of the building together. Alberto was helping support Mateo, who was now walking with a cane. Many more tears flowed.

There were nonstop hugs and kisses back and forth between Ricardo and his family. Ricardo introduced each of them to the general, and Marta was so overwhelmed and excited that instead of shaking the general's hand she put her arms around him and kissed him on both cheeks. The general was surprised by Marta's behavior, but graciously kissed her cheeks in return.

General de Longa then bowed to Mateo saying, "I am honored to meet you Señor Vasquez. You are a hero to our Spanish people."

A humbled, yet happy Mateo, responded, "The honor is mine, General de Longa."

Marta kept pinching herself to be certain this happy reunion was not a dream.

Everyone went upstairs to the Columbo's apartment where Marta insisted on making dinner for all of them, including a special apple treat for Bataar.

Chapter Forty-Four
Treasures from the Journey

ater that night, the family and Mateo gathered around the dinner table. As he took each item from his pack, Ricardo told a brief story about its significance. He began with the carved spoon from the captain of the Aviela, followed by the Mandinke amulet from Martim, and the palm seed from Ali. He showed them the Qadamy, the Silk Road Flyer, the poop collector and the key to the city of Antioch.

They were all impressed when Ricardo told them he was a student of yoga. They let out a collective "ooh" when he showed them his needles and said that he was an expert in acupuncture, even though none of them had ever heard of it before.

"These are from the emperor of China," Ricardo said proudly. "This is a gold paiza. It is a passport that allowed us to travel from country to country along the Silk Road. And my friend, the emperor, gave me this carved statue of a dragon. I think I will give it to our king when we see him tomorrow.

"Mother, the emperor of China sent this especially to you. He sent a note for you as well."

Marta screamed with joy when she opened the velvet box and saw the beautiful ruby and gold bracelet.

"Is it real?"

"Yes, Mother, it is!"

Ricardo then took out the stack of Chinese *chao*.

"Father, you can use some of this money to open the Columbo Family Pharmacy you have always dreamed about."

More tears followed.

"I would like the rest of the chao to go you, Señor

Vasquez, so you may live the rest of your years in comfort."

Mateo tried to thank Ricardo, but he couldn't get the words out between his tears.

Ricardo turned to Anna and Esteban as he lifted the jade necklace from his pack.

"I want to use this to fund a wonderful education for both of you at the best schools in Spain. It was given to me by the Sultan of Delhi in India in gratitude for some advice I gave him."

After tucking Anna and Esteban into bed and saying goodnight to Mateo, Ricardo sat down with his mother and father. He pulled out the page from Exodus that Professor Jatoo had given him and the Tallit from Rabbi Yosef and Sarah. Ricardo looked into his parents' eyes and asked, "Please tell me, are we Jewish? There were so many signs and feelings on my journey that led me to believe we are."

There was a long period of silence before his father answered.

"We are indeed Jewish, Ricardo. Our Jewish blood goes back for centuries. In fact, your great-grandfather, my grandpa, was a rabbi. Our family is from Toledo, Spain. Toledo was a center of Jewish life until there was a period of terrible discrimination against us. We moved to Madrid and never told anyone here that we were Jewish. We kept our Jewish heritage a secret so Anna, Esteban and you could grow up without knowing the prejudice and fear that we experienced."

"What happened to our grandparents?" Ricardo asked. "I have a few memories of them, like at Passover, but that is all."

Ricardo's mother looked down at the floor, took a deep breath, and looked back up to Ricardo.

"They were taken from us in a riot against Jews. We never heard from them again. That was when we moved here."

Unable to contain her emotion any longer, Ricardo's mother began to cry.

"We are so sorry, Ricardo."

"Mother and Father, I want to learn about my Jewish heritage. Please tell me everything you can remember."

Alberto went to a closet and pulled out a very old book from under a pile of linens.

"Here is a good place to start. This was my father's prayer book. I can teach you to read Hebrew, if you wish."

"Mother," Ricardo asked, "does the symbol on the note you put in my jacket pocket mean something about being Jewish?" חי

"Yes Ricardo, it does. It is the Hebrew word *chai*, which means *life*. Its letters are the eighth and tenth letters of the Hebrew alphabet. Together they add up to eighteen, which is the number we Jews believe represents good luck and long life."

The following morning, Ricardo, his family and Señor Vasquez met with Peter of Castile at his palace. After a ceremony to honor Mateo, Ricardo presented the king with the jeweled dragon statue as a gift from the emperor of China. The king was so excited about the gift and learning about all of Ricardo's experiences that he asked Ricardo to be one of his foreign policy advisers on the Far East.

On their way home from the palace, Ricardo showed his

family and Señor Vasquez the spectacular diamond Chief Hin had given him.

"I helped the chief's son," Ricardo explained, lightly shrugging one of his shoulders.

His mother fainted!

Chapter Forty-Five
Islas Canarias

In a courtroom in Madrid, ambassadors from the Kingdom of Portugal, the Crown of Spain, and the Kingdom of Genoa met before justices from each of their respective countries. The Chief Justice, Alfonso Santos from Portugal, opened the proceedings.

"My fellow justices, we are here to determine which of our three countries has the right to the Canary Islands. Should they be known as the *Spanish Islas Canarias*, the *Genoaese Isola Canarino*, or the *Portuguese Ilhas Canaria*? Since our three countries are friends and allies in our upcoming struggle against Peter IV of Aragon and the Kingdom of France, it is fitting that our nations settle this territorial dispute peacefully in a court of law.

"The Honorable Ambassador of Spain has requested to be the first to present his case to the court. Mr. Ambassador..."

"Thank you, Your Honor. May it please the court that I call my first and only witness, Señor Mateo Vasquez," spoke the Ambassador to Spain.

Although Mateo was nearing his nineties and used a cane, he walked like a soldier with a strong stride and military posture, to the witness box.

"Please state your name and your occupation," said the clerk of the court.

"Mateo Vasquez, former explorer for the Crown of Spain," responded Mateo.

"To get right to the point, Señor Vasquez, are you familiar with Islas Canarias?" asked the Ambassador.

"Yes, I am. I claimed them for Spain more than sixty years ago," Mateo spoke decisively.

There was a murmur in the courtroom.

"And how can you say that so confidently, Señor

Vasquez?" asked the Ambassador.

"Because, sir, it is true. My men and I claimed them. Unfortunately, my men are all dead and gone now," answered Mateo.

"So do you expect us to simply take your word on this critical matter? Is there any way you can prove your claim?"

"Yes, there is, Your Excellency. Have you heard of the language used by the natives of those islands, the *Guanches*?" Mateo asked.

"I have heard of it. It is called *El Silbo* and is a strange whistled version of Spanish. It transposes a Spanish form of speech to whistling, if I understand correctly."

"You are indeed correct. It is based on an ancient language the natives used to whistle so they could communicate over the ravines and valleys of the islands. When we first came to the islands, they used it mostly to exchange messages, for example, to warn their fellow islanders of an incoming storm or an enemy attack. They could send the messages reverberating for up to five kilometers.

"I befriended several of the Guanches chiefs and taught

them to expand their whistling language into a basic version of Spanish. It greatly increased their vocabulary and their ability to communicate. It brought the natives closer together and it is still used today," Mateo explained.

"That is an interesting story, Señor Vasquez. How do we know it is true?" the Ambassador asked.

Mateo Vasquez rose from his chair and proceeded to whistle a message in El Silbo quite clearly and strongly.

From the back of the courtroom came another whistle, which Ricardo thought was an echo at first. But then he spied a wrinkled old man being helped to his feet by a middle-aged man and a young girl.

Señor Vasquez faced the judges and said, "Your Honors, may I present Chief Mency Bencomo of the Guanches people of *Islas Canarias*. He is accompanied by his son Enrique and his granddaughter Nuria."

The three islanders nodded to the judges. Señor Vasquez whistled a message to them in El Silbo and they replied.

Then the chief's son spoke to the judges in Spanish. "Thank you for allowing three generations of Guanches to appear before your court. My father would like to speak to you in our native language, El Silbo. His granddaughter will translate his words for you."

Chief Bencomo whistled for several minutes, pausing occasionally so Nuria could repeat his words in Spanish. This is what he said: "We are Guanches from Islas Canairias. I met Señor Vasquez many years ago when he landed on our islands. He understood that were a proud people. He helped us merge our cultures. Señor Vasquez is our friend. Our Guanches children and grandchildren speak both Spanish and El Silbo, and we plan to teach both languages to our future generations. We are loyal citizens of Spain and wish to remain so."

There was a stunned silence in the courtroom. Then, after conferring with the other judges, the Chief Justice spoke, "Señor Vasquez and his friends have made the case for Spain. No other countries need to be heard. Islas Canarias belong to Spain. This case is closed."

A cheer went up throughout the courtroom audience, which included Peter of Castile and the entire Columbo family.

As they exited the courtroom, Ricardo's mind was racing with ideas about how he could build upon the many experiences he had during his travel adventures. He thought he might open a yoga studio, heal patients with acupuncture he learned in China, or even sell his ingenious poop collector. Whatever his path might eventually take, he was certain that helping others, particularly those who may be less fortunate than he, would always be an integral part of his life. And to think, if he had never left Spain...he might never have opened his eyes to the world around him and all of its possibilities.

EPILOGUE

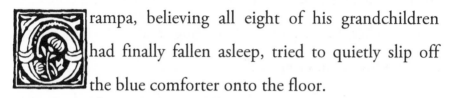rampa, believing all eight of his grandchildren had finally fallen asleep, tried to quietly slip off the blue comforter onto the floor.

"Gumpa," asked Rachel, "what happened to Mercy? I really liked her."

"So did I," added Yael.

"Gramps, is Bataar still alive?" asked Lev.

David pressed, "When we visit you next time, can you tell us another Ricardo story?"

"Please Grampa," pleaded Shira and Michal. "Pretty please, Grampa," echoed Aviva and Esther.

"Well," Grampa replied, "Ricardo's adventures didn't end when he was sixteen. Of course, there is more. But if you would really like to hear about Ricardo's other adventures, I guess you will have to wait until the next time you visit. I have to warn you, though, some of that story might make you sad…and mad."

The children went silent, their smiles replaced by furrowed brows and frowns.

"…But excited and very happy, too!" Grampa laughed, finishing his sentence as his grandchildren let out a collective sigh of relief, followed by cheers, hugs and a glorious chorus of, "We love you, Grampa!"

"Now go to sleep, because we are all going to the zoo in the morning," he said with a smile as he closed the door.

Grampa walked back to his bedroom, opened his dresser drawer and reverently picked up the ancient map and the tattered 800-year-old Hebrew prayer book. He held them next to his heart and thought how important and beautiful his family and his heritage were to him.

Placing the map and the holy book back in the dresser drawer, he whispered softly, "Until next time."

Grampa then fell into a deep and satisfying sleep, dreaming of his ancestor Ricardo's many adventures.

ABOUT THE AUTHOR

An entrepreneur and business and non-profit consultant, Richard Bergman has written several wonderful children's books. Passionate about giving back to the community, he is a co-founder of *Embracing Our Differences* and is actively involved in several other non-profit organizations, including *The Jewish Federation of Sarasota-Manatee, Child Protection Center*, and *Tickets for Kids*. Most significantly, Rich is "Grampa" to his beloved grandchildren, to whom he seeks to transmit his deep rooted family values and traditions that came from his grandfather. Rich and his wife Rebecca reside in Sarasota, Florida, and together they have five children and eight grandchildren.

APPENDIX A

Foods by Chapter

Chapter 4 - The Aviela

1. **Thousand-year-old eggs**- duck eggs preserved in ash and salt for 100 days. Turns grey and looks ancient. Very salty. From China.

2. **Kao rou**- Barbeque meat. From Burma.

3. **Kutt hu roti**- Deep fried bread filled with vegetables, eggs and meat. From Ceylon.

4. **Escamol**e- Edible larvae and pupae of ants. From Mexico.

5. **Eri polu**- Cooked pupas of silk worms. From India.

6. **Phan pyat**- Rotted potatoes and spices. From Viet Nam.

7. **Stargazey pie**- Pie made from potatoes, eggs and sardines. Often has fish heads sticking out from the crust. From Celtic Britain.

8. **Mascarpone cream**- Whipping cream, mascarpone cheese, vanilla and sugar mixed. From Italy.

9. **Gazpacho**- cold soup made of raw blended vegetables.

From Spain and Portugal.

10. **Paella-** Rice dish, cooked over an open fire. Often with mussels or clams. From Spain.

Chapter 8 - The Jungle

1. **Poulet yassa-** Spicy chicken with lemons and onions. From Senegal, Africa.

2. **Tigadegena-** Peanut stew with chicken, potatoes, peanut butter. From Mali, Africa.

3. **Meni-meniyong-** Sesame and honey sweet bar. From Mali, Africa.

4. **Baobob-** Fruit from "Monkey Bread tree". Very nutritious. From Africa.

Chapter 24....Giona and Anika

1. **Palak chaat-** Fried spinach with yogurt and chutney. From India.

2. **Tandoori lamb-** Lamb roasted in a tandoor clay oven marinated with yogurt and spices. From India.

3. **Naan, kulcha and roti-** Various breads. From India.

Chapter 26 - The Trip to China

Jiuniang- Fermented soup made with sweet rice wine.

From China.

Chapter 29 - The Emperor

Rich and Noble chicken (also called Beggar's Chicken)- Whole chicken stuffed with nuts, mushrooms and a blend of spices slowly cooked for up to six hours. From China.

Chapter 33 - The Chinese New Year

1. **Jaozi**- Wheat dough dumpling filled with pork or vegetables. Served for the Chinese New Year. From China.

2. **Niangao**- Steamed Chinese New Year sweet rice cake. From China.

Chapter 35 - Mongolia

1. **Airag**- Fermented horse milk From Mongolia.

2. **Buuz**- Steamed dumplings filled with meat From Mongolia.

Chapter 36 - The Yam and the Silk Road

1. **Osh plov**- Lamb dish with rice, onions, carrots and garlic. From Uzbekistan.

2. **Maida manti**- Squares of dough filed with potatoes and spices. From Uzbekistan.

3. **Mega-samsa**- Flaky pastry filled with potatoes and meat,

topped with sesame seeds. From Uzbekistan.

4. **Lepyoshka**- Thick flat bread baked in Obi Nan clay ovens. From Afghanistan.

5. **Gondi Nokhodchi**- Chicken meat balls from Persia/Iran.

6. **Gondi Kashi**- Rice with turkey, fava beans, beets and herbs from Persia/Iran.

7. **Challah**- Traditional Jewish braided bread, typically served on the Sabbath and on major Jewish holidays. The simple dough is made of eggs, water, flour, yeast, and salt and has a rich flavor. From Israel and the Diaspora.

Chapter 38 - Constantinople

Garum- Fermented fish sauce. From Greece, Rome and Byzantine Empire.

Chapter 40 - Rome

1. **Suppli**- Risotto with Chicken, cheese and a tomato sauce. From Italy.

2. **Flora dizucca**- Fried stuffed zucchini flowers. From Italy.

3. **Baccala**- Baked salted cod with tomatoes, olive oil, and peppers. From Italy.

APPENDIX B

Cities and Sites Ricardo Visited

1. Madrid, Spain

2. Mamsar, Guinea

3. Timbuktu, Mali

4. Sahara Desert, North Africa

   Zizi Oasis

5. Cairo, Egypt

6. Jerusalem, Israel

   The Wall

   Temple Mount

   Citadel

   Al Asqa Mosque

   Church of the Holy Sepulcher

   Fourteen Stations of the Cross

   Tower of David

   Mount of Olives

7. Red Sea

8. Indian Ocean

9. Bay of Bengal

10. Saptagram, India - historical port city of Southern Bengal, India. Some call it the origin of Calcutta (Kolkata).

11. Ganges River, India

12. Strait of Malacca

13. China Sea

14. Hangzhou, China

15. Grand Canal, China

16. Dadu, China - as the capital of the Yuan dynasty and the main center of the Mongol Empire founded by Kublai Khan. Today it is China's capital, Beijing.

17. Shaanxi, China
    Terra Cotta Army

18. Great Wall of China, China

19. Xanadu, Mongolia

20. Lanzhou, China

21. Kashgar, China

22. Osh, Kyrgyzstan

23. Bahlika, Afghanistan

24. Bukhara, Uzbekistan

25. Merv, Turkmenistan

26. Hamandan, Iran

    Ali Sadr Cave

    Tomb of Avicenna [Canon of Medicine]

    Tomb of Esther and Mordechai

27. Antioch, Turkey

28. Constantinople, Turkey

29. Straits of Bosphoros

30. Aegean Sea

31. Mediterranean Sea

32. Rome, Italy

    Colosseum

    Roman Forum

    Arch of Titus

    Seven Hills of Rome

    Tiber River

33. Avignon, France

    Pont Saint Benezel Bridge

34. Nimes, France

Maison Caree Roman Temple

Pont di Gard Bridge

Magne Tower

35. Cerebere, France

36. Pontbou, Spain

37. Guadalajara, Spain

Castillo de Zafra Castle

38. Canary islands, Spanish Archipelago* [reason for trial]

39. Madrid, Spain

APPENDIX C

Things to Know

1. **Acupuncture (zhenjiiu)**- is based on the premise that a blockage or disturbance in the flow of the body's life energy, or "qi," causes health issues. By inserting hair-thin needles into specific acupuncture points throughout the body to restore the flow of qi, acupuncturists believe they restore the body's energy, stimulate healing, and promote relaxation.

2. **Animism** - the religious belief that a supernatural spiritual power resides in all things: animals, plants, rocks, even words.

3. **Asserrin, Asserran** - old Spanish nursery rhyme/ children's song. Translates to "the carpenter swept the sawdust off the floor of the workshop."

4. **Bhagavad Gita** - referred to as the Gita, it is a 700-verse Sanskrit scripture that is part of the Hindu epic Mahabharata. The Bhagavad-Gita is the eternal message of spiritual wisdom from ancient India, and is also called "the

song of God."

5. **Brahmin** - a class in Hinduism specializing as priests, teachers, and protectors of sacred learning across generations. The Brahmins were the highest ranking social class.

6. **Canary Islands** - in Spanish, Islas Canarias, is an archipelago and the southernmost autonomous community of Spain. It is located in the Atlantic Ocean.

7. **Chi** – a traditional Chinese unit of length, often called the "Chinese foot."

8. **Dom** - the Gypsies (some consider this to be a derogatory term) of the Middle East call themselves Dom, which means "man" in their native Domari language. There are an estimated 1,000 Dom living in Jerusalem's Old City.

9. **El Silbo** - is a whistled register of Spanish used by inhabitants of La Gomera in the Canary Islands to communicate across the deep ravines and narrow valleys that radiate through the island. It is a transposition of Spanish from speech to whistling.

10. **Ganges River** - flows through India and Bangladesh. The

2,525 kilometer Ganges is one of the most sacred rivers to Hindus. It is also a lifeline to millions of Indians who live along its course and depend on it for their daily needs. The Ganges is highly polluted.

11. **Genghis Kahn** - was the founder of the Mongol Empire. He united many nomadic tribes in Asia.

12. **Guanches** - were the aboriginal inhabitants of the Canary Islands. After the Spanish conquest of the Canaries they were culturally absorbed by Spanish settlers, although elements of their culture survive to this day, such as "El Silbo" (the whistled language of La Gomera Island).

13. **Gypsy** – (some consider this to be a derogatory term) a person of Roma descent, a nomadic ethnic group originating from areas near India. The Roma do not follow a single faith; rather, they often adopt the predominant religion of the country where they are living, and describe themselves as "many stars scattered in the sight of God."

14. **King Hezikiah** - the 13th king of Judah, prominently mentioned in the Hebrew Bible.

15. **Kublai Kahn** - was the grandson of Genghis Khan.

Kublai established the Yuan dynasty, which ruled over present-day Mongolia, China, and Korea. Kublai became the first non-Han emperor to conquer all of China.

16. **Kumbh Mela** - is a pilgrimage of faith in which Hindus gather to bathe in a sacred or holy river once every twelve years. The main festival site is located on the banks of a river, example: the Ganges. Bathing in these rivers is thought to cleanse a person of all their sins.

17. **Manden** - The Great Mali Empire in West Africa from circa 1235 - 1400. The empire became renowned for the wealth of its rulers, especially Mansa Musa.

18. **Patriarch Kallistos I** - was the Ecumenical Patriarch of Constantinople in the mid 1300s.

19. **Peter of Castile** - also called "Peter the Cruel" and "Peter the Just" was the king of Castile and León, Spain from 1350 to 1369.

20. **Qadamy** – a game involving kicking a small object back and forth without letting it touch the ground, derived from the Arab word for "foot."

21. **Salute and Cin Cin** - the Italians say "cheers" in two

ways. "Salute" is used in an informal situation or "Cin cin" in a more formal context. Some great Italian drinking toasts or cheers, besides salute, are "cento di questi giorni" (May you have 100 of these days), and "cent' anni" (100 years).

22. **Salt Trade** - camel caravans from North Africa carried bars of salt as well as cloth, tobacco, and metal tools across the Sahara to trading centers like Djenne and Timbuktu on the Niger River. Some items for which the salt was traded include gold, ivory, slaves, skins, kola nuts, pepper, and sugar.

23. **Savannah** - a tropical grassland, as in parts of Africa, containing scattered trees and drought-resistant undergrowth.

24. **Shamanism** – a religion that involves reaching altered states of consciousness in order to interact with the spirit world and channel those energies into this world.

25. **Silk Road** - was an ancient network of trade routes that connected the East and the West (Asia, Africa and Europe). The Silk Road derived its name from the expan-

sive trading of silk along its route.

26. **Sultan of Delhi** - at one time, he controlled much of the Indian subcontinent. The sultanate is noted for being one of the few states to repel an attack by the Mongols and was once led by one of the few female rulers in Islamic history.

27. **Sun Tzu** - was a Chinese military strategist who lived in ancient China. He was the author of *The Art of War*, an influential work that has affected Western and East Asian philosophy and military thinking. Sun Tzu is revered in Chinese culture as a legendary historical and military figure.

28. **The Book of Genesis** - "In the beginning" is the first book of the Hebrew Bible and the Old Testament. Tradition credits Moses as the author of Genesis.

29. **The Plague** - also known as the Great Plague or the Black Death, was one of the most devastating pandemics of all time, resulting in the deaths of an estimated 75 to 200 million people in Europe and Asia. The Black Death is thought to have originated in Asia, where it travelled

along the Silk Road. It was most likely carried by fleas living on the rats on merchant ships.

30. **The Sahara** - the Great Desert is located on the African continent. It is the largest hot desert in the world. Its area is comparable to the area of China or the United States. The name "Sahara" is derived from an Arabic word for desert.

31. **Toghon Temur, Emperor** - the last emperor of the Yuan Dynasty in China.

32. **War of Two Peters** - was fought from 1356 to 1375 between the kingdoms of Castile and Aragon. Its name refers to the rulers of the countries, both named Peter.

33. **Yam** - a supply and postal system used by Genghis Kahn and by subsequent Great Kahns. Relay stations provided food, shelter and spare horses to Mongol soldiers and messengers.

34. **Ying Zheng or Qin Shi Huang** - was the founder of the Qin dynasty and the first emperor of a unified China. During his reign, his generals greatly expanded the size of the Chinese state.

35.**Zoroastrianism** - one of the world's oldest active religions. It is monotheistic and revolves around the battle between good and evil. In the end, they believe, that evil will be destroyed.

Appendix D

Hebrew/ Yiddish Words

1. **B'Sheret**- a Yiddish word meaning "destiny" or "meant to be." Also can refer to your "soulmate" as your B'Sheret.

2. **Chai**- Hebrew for "life."

3. **L'Chaim**...a Yiddish expression meaning "to life," often used during toasts and celebrations.

4. **Mazel Tov**- Hebrew for "good luck," or "I am pleased this good thing has happened to you, "or "congratulations."

5. **Mitzvah**- Hebrew word for "Commandment," Also refers to acts of human kindness, moral deeds.

6. **Pesach**- Hebrew name for Passover. Holiday in which Jews commemorate their liberation from slavery in ancient Egypt under the leadership of Moses.

7. **Purim**- A joyous Jewish holiday that commemorates when Jews in Persia were saved by the heroic actions of Queen Esther and Mordechai.

8. **Seder-** a ritual feast that marks the beginning of the Jewish holiday of Passover. It involves the retelling of the story of the Exodus from Egypt.

9. **Shabbat-** Hebrew for "Sabbath." Shabbat begins on Friday at nightfall and lasts until nightfall on Saturday. Stems from the Hebrew word "rest."

10. **Tallit-** Hebrew for "prayer shawl."

11. **Tikkun Olam-** Hebrew for "repair the world," has come to mean action for social justice.

12. **Tisha B'Av** - is an annual fasting day in Judaism commemorating the destruction of Solomon's Temple and the Second Temple. Tisha B'Av is regarded as the saddest day in the Jewish calendar.

Appendix E

Illustrations

CPSIA information can be obtained
at www.ICGtesting.com
Printed in the USA
BVHW081448221119
564522BV00001B/43/P